ANDREW BRAEMAN

AF192134

# THE
# STONYPOOL
## CURSE

novum ◢ pro

This book is also available as e-book.

© 2024 novum publishing

ISBN 978-3-99146-921-6
Editing: Gillian Fisher
Cover photo:
Zoom-zoom I Dreamstime.com
Cover design, layout & typesetting:
novum publishing

**www.novum-publishing.co.uk**

Print product with financial
**climate contribution**
ClimatePartner.com/16547-2311-1001

# Contents

# The Stonypool Curse

A small English seaside town,
late October, 1970

# Chapter 1

## Day One

I'm sure that for many of us, a typical English seaside town is somewhere we love to be, with its slightly dated facades, everything needed for a day on the beach there for the purchasing, from buckets and spades to newspapers and ice creams. A certain magic exists. But come autumn, when traders have shut up shop and holidaymakers are a distant memory, a strange melancholy descends. Stonypool is just such a town. Only in that late autumn, it wasn't only melancholy that descended; it was accompanied by evil.

The season was well and truly over in Stonypool. Even Moira Taggart, who ran the tiny museum that nestled between a chip shop and an amusement arcade, had pulled down the shutters. That place was her life and Moira Taggart was a museum piece herself now. Approaching ninety, and thirty years a widow, she took up a stick from behind the counter, turned off the lights, unhooked her coat from the coat rack and slipping it on went out into the now dark autumn afternoon. 'She'll not be here next year' was heard among Stonypool traders every year. But back she came, a little more stooped, a little more deaf. That had been her twenty-fifth season.

What is to be found in Mrs Taggart 's museum? A reasonable question. Artefacts from the town's past, old photographs – many of significant local events – artefacts from local shipwrecks, personal effects of long-dead mariners, and a rather out-of-place collection of witch bottles and other items intended to ward off evil that had been recovered from the many fishermen's cottages when they were demolished to make way for the grand Victorian villas and hotels that were to follow.

Moira locked the door, trying the handle three times to ensure it was indeed locked: a twenty-five-year-old habit. She turned to face the sea, but with failing hearing, she didn't hear the crash from inside the museum. Neither did she see the peculiar purple glow that permeated from within. Tonight, those artefacts intended for the warding off of evil would have their work cut out for them.

Almost directly opposite, the bald and rotund pier manager, Dennis Rawlson, stood by the pay kiosk, inhaling heavily on a cigar. It had been a good summer and he was more than ready for a break. The pier had been in safe hands since he had taken over. A well-liked individual, Dennis held a place on the local council and gave generously to local charities. There was but one flaw in his otherwise settled life: his somewhat turbulent marriage of thirty years to his wife, Rita. Locking the turnstile behind him, he made his way along the now darkened pier, checking doors, and making sure that the piles of deckchairs were firmly strapped down. The only guests now were the seagulls and it seemed to Dennis that even they were fewer this year. He wandered into the central amusement arcade, the machines now lifeless. Three widely spaced ceiling-hung light bulbs provided the only illumination. It failed to attract his attention how they swung on this day when there was no wind and the sea was flat calm.

Exiting at the other end of the arcade, he progressed a few yards to the entrance of the End of the Pier Theatre. It was his pride and joy. He had kept it faithful to its Victorian origins. On many afternoons in the summer its two hundred seats were filled. He relit his cigar, opened the doors and proceeded, with the assistance of the emergency lighting, through the foyer to the entrance to the auditorium where on the left there was a small cupboard that contained switches for the house lighting. A second later the auditorium was flooded with light. For a few moments Dennis looked on with pride before turning back to the switch panel. Had he looked up, he would have seen what resembled the limp body of a young man hanging from the gallery above, swinging like those light bulbs in the arcade, which seconds later had faded away. Was it the thought of going home to his wife that was making him feel strangely angry, or was it something he had no control over?

Meanwhile, outside the pier entrance, Madame Volatska, real name Mary Sharp, the fortune-teller, had returned to her tiny kiosk to collect things that needed to be taken home and kept dry for the winter. As she locked the door for the last time that year, she looked across the promenade and noticed the glow emanating from Moira Taggart's museum. However, she thought little of it, assuming that Moira was still in residence. Mary was never surprised at the things Moira got up to in that place after closing. But, had she looked back before leaving, she would have seen a girl, no more than eleven or twelve years old, dressed in a white summer dress and completely drenched, her long dark hair hanging lank around a paper-white face, who soon faded away.

Two hundred yards to the west of the pier, the landlord of the Ship and Anchor public house was bottling up in the bar, although he was not expecting a busy evening. Only locals this time of year. Ken Lomes was a generally happy and contented but sometimes ill tempered man, although his permanent hang-dog expression and deep-set eyes made him look anything but. He was sure his best friend, Dennis Rawlson, would be in that night for his two pints of Dutch courage before going home to his wife. Ken had heard everything there was to hear about Dennis' disastrous marriage over the years, although he didn't believe it could be as bad as Dennis made out. After all, he had met Rita Rawlson many times and always found her an attractive but somewhat coarse woman who could quickly irritate him. And she had a propensity to appear in public somewhat overly made-up. As Ken served the first customers of the evening, he failed to hear the sound of a glass smashing behind the counter of the empty saloon bar.

A short distance to the east of the pier stands the Beach View Hotel, and behind the counter stood Tara Jones. In her late twenties, she looked a little older – in fact very much the seaside landlady. It was the start of Tara's first winter season since taking over Beach View Hotel. It had been a busy summer and she was grateful for the quieter days of autumn. There were only three guests in residence: a young couple from London, who were there for a family wedding, and a young female sales representative in town on business.

Soon, however, the guest count would be reduced by one as the lone female arrived at the reception desk, complaining of disturbing occurrences in her room earlier, and that morning she had reported knocking coming from the floors and walls, objects moving, and the ceiling light seemingly having a mind of its own. If she had looked back as she fled the room forever, she would have seen the lifeless body of a woman lying upon the bed, a trickle of blood at her right wrist, eyes wide open, fixed in a startled stare, who seconds later faded away.

A young couple were walking arm in arm along the promenade. They were clearly very much in love. And as is often said, love is blind, and in this case it was true. They failed to notice the young man staggering in a ginnel between two shops, a knife sticking out from his back, who, a moment later, faded away.

What everyone also seemingly failed to notice was the peculiar purple hue of the sky above the long disused Empire Ballroom. The Empire Ballroom had opened in the late 1800s as the Victoria Dance Hall. For over 80 years, it had welcomed the young and old of Stonypool for nights of dancing and entertainment – before Bingo became the trend – followed by closure when the leaseholders, facing financial difficulty, could no longer honour the terms of the full maintenance lease. Since then, decay and vandalism had taken its toll. It had a reputation among the local population for being haunted, as so often old and disused buildings do. What they didn't know was the secret the Empire Ballroom had kept so well concealed for so long.

Was that the reason why vagrant Frank Chapley, who usually slept inside, behind the unlocked and open back doors at the rear of the ballroom, now chose to sleep outside and face the ravages of the autumnal weather? Later that night, Frank could be seen running, putting as much distance as possible between himself and the old ballroom. And if he had turned to look back, he would maybe have been the first to notice that peculiar light in the sky above the building. That evening was just the start of so much strangeness.

## Chapter 2

### Day Two

Dennis Rawlson awoke, as was his habit, at seven o'clock. He showered, took his dressing gown from the chair by the bed, and slipping it on went to the window and opened the curtains to be greeted by a dull and damp morning. He turned away in disgust at the sight of a dead seagull on his balcony, its head torn from its shoulders.

Rita Rawlson awoke. It was clear her mood was less than good.

'Dennis, you woke me. You said last night that you would lie in as the season's over. I won't get back to sleep now. And what are you looking at on the balcony?

Dennis smiled. 'Death, my dear. Death!'

'You speak in riddles, Dennis. Go and make me a cup of tea. And I don't want you under my feet all day. Go and find something to do. Constructive, mind, not the Ship and Anchor.

Dennis' smile grew broader, but Rita could not see. 'Yes, dear. Absolutely.' But he was thinking, *of course I'll go to the Ship and Anchor*.

By eight o'clock, Dennis had left a dishevelled and nagging Rita sitting at the kitchen table as he made his way out onto the street. Outside, a light drizzle was falling. There was something wrong, Dennis could sense it. The clouds, flat, grey, obscuring the sky, had a strange purple-orange hue. The air seemed thick, heavy. It wasn't particularly cold. There was a peculiar smell carried on the slight breeze.

He stepped on something soft that crunched under his weight. He looked down and gagged. Another headless seagull. He raised his head. Before him, along the High Street, were thirty, forty, maybe fifty dead – and so far as he could tell – headless seagulls, which, as he made his way towards the seafront, is what he realised they were. Recovering from the initial shock, a thought came into his mind that this was going to be a somewhat difficult clean-up operation for the town council, and that questions would be asked by the committee as to how it had happened.

At the end of the High Street, near the seafront, Dennis turned left, and seconds later he stood rooted to the spot outside the Empire Ballroom. Was it his imagination or was that a scream he had heard from within the once grand venue? He stood, his senses sharp. Another scream, the sound of which he could only reconcile as women crying. Then came a series of loud bangs. Then silence.

At the Ship and Anchor, Ken Lomes was standing behind the bar, tidying. He wasn't expecting much custom that day, but he liked everything to be in order. Having restocked the shelves in the public bar, he walked through to the saloon bar, pausing at the sight that greeted him. Behind the bar was a sea of broken glass. He looked at the shelf above the bar. Not a glass to be seen. The sturdy shelf was intact, not leaning at some precarious angle. For a while he just stood and stared, not knowing quite the best way to deal with what he had encountered. And as he stood and contemplated, there was a furious knocking upon the front door.

Ken called out, 'We're closed!'

In reply came a muffled voice he recognised. 'Ken, it's Dennis. Let me in quick!'

Ken ran to the door, turned keys in locks, and opened it. A clearly distressed Dennis Rawlson burst in.

'Ken, fetch me a brandy. Fast!'

Madame Volatska, aka Mary Sharp, fortune-teller, awoke later than was usual for her. She had not set her alarm clock. After all, there was nowhere she needed to be. Prising herself from her bed, she slipped on her dressing gown and made her way to the kitchen. Crossing the threshold, she put a foot on the tiled floor, and stepped into a freezing cold pool of water. Her immediate reaction was to look up at the ceiling, expecting to see damage from a burst pipe. Nothing. Stepping over the puddle, she filled the kettle and switched it on to boil. Then she took a tea towel to place over the puddle, and on hands and knees she began to mop it up, unaware that behind her stood the drowned girl who had appeared at the pier the night before.

The telephone rang.

At the Ship and Anchor, Dennis Rawlson had begun to feel more himself after two large brandies, and was trying to reconcile the events of the morning in his mind by explaining them to the ever-understanding landlord.

'So, Ken, what do you think? Strange, eh?'

'I think you'd better come and have a look at this, Dennis.' Ken led the way to the saloon bar, lifted the latch and beckoned for Dennis to go behind the bar with him.

'Blimey, Ken! What happened? Angry customer?' Dennis chuckled.

'In some way, Dennis, I wish it was. At least then there would be an explanation.'

'Fetch a dustpan and brush, Ken. I'll give you a hand to clean it up. So, you really have no idea how this happened?'

The telephone rang in the hallway of the living accommodation and the answering machine, Ken's new pride and joy, cut in:

'Hello. This is Ken Lomes, landlord of the Ship and Anchor. I can't get to the phone right now, so please leave your message after the tone.'

'It's Rita. Rita Rawlson. If my useless husband is there – and I'm sure he is – tell him he's in big trouble!'

At the back of the Empire Ballroom, two young boys stood at the open doors, daring each other to go inside. Tim Marks and David Rudd, typical boys, and always pushing boundaries.

'Go inside, Tim,' quipped David.

'No. You go inside, David. I'll give you half of my week's pocket money if you do.'

Of course, he had no intention of doing that, but the somewhat gullible David agreed. Pushing the doors further open, David stared into the darkness then took a few steps inside, rubble and broken glass crunching under foot. As his eyes grew accustomed to the dark, he took a few more steps, then tripped over something on the floor. He fell, landing on something soft. Reaching down he felt what he thought was a bundle of rags, but as he searched, his right hand encountered what could only be a bearded face. He jumped up in horror and screamed, alerting Tim to his distress.

'David! Are you okay?'

'No! There's a dead man in here!'

Madame Volatska lifted the receiver of her telephone. 'Hello.'

'Is that Mary, Mary Sharp?

'It is. Who's calling?'

'It's your nephew, Craig. Craig Norton.'

'Craig? It must be ten years since I last spoke to you!'

'At least that, Mary. Listen, I'm coming down your way. I was wondering if I could stay with you. Just for a few days?'

'Of course you can, Craig. I'd enjoy the company to be honest. When are you planning to come?'

'This afternoon if that's okay? I'm planning to catch the twelve o'clock train, so I should be there by two thirty.'

'That soon! Fine with me. Can I ask what you're coming down for?'

'Something tells me I'm going to be needed, Mary. I assume you're still living at the same place?'

'Yes, I am. Needed for what?'

'I'll explain when I see you. Is everything alright there? Nothing unusual happened?'

'Well, only what I thought was a leak in the kitchen, big pool of water, you know. But it turns out it isn't.'

'I definitely need to get to you. Bye. And thanks, Mary. See you later.'

At the Beach View Hotel, the young couple, the only remaining guests, were at the reception desk to check out.

'We've had a lovely stay, Miss Jones, but I think you might have vermin in the wall cavities. Terrible scratching all night. Oh, and I do apologise, but we found one of the bedside lamps on the floor this morning. The shade is damaged. I'm sure it wasn't us, but of course I'm very happy to pay for the damage.'

Tara Jones smiled. 'No, I've been meaning to replace them anyway. I do apologise if you had a disturbed night. I'm pleased you enjoyed your stay.'

There was a crash from upstairs. The three turned their heads at the same instant towards the staircase.

Two distressed boys, Tim Marks and David Rudd, stood at the counter of the front office of Stonypool Police Station, explaining their grisly find to PC Steve Bardon, the local beat constable.

'A body you say? In the old Empire Ballroom?'

'Well, that's what David said it was. I only looked from a distance,' remarked Tim.

PC Bardon took his jacket from the stand behind the desk.

'Well, we'd better go and take a look. I think I'll take the Panda car though.'

Despite the shock of that morning, the thought of a ride in a police car brought a smile to the boys' faces.

At the Ship and Anchor, Dennis and Ken had cleared the last of the glass from behind the saloon bar.

'Listen, Ken, I'm not going home. Rita is clearly in a foul mood.'

'I gathered that, Dennis. You can stay here if you like.'

'I could, or we could go over to the pier and have a few rounds of cards in the theatre?'

'Sounds good to me, Dennis. My new barmaid, Julie, will be here soon and it's not going to be a busy day anyway. It'll be good to see how she copes on her own.'

'Perfect! Grab a bottle of whisky and bring your cash. You're going to need it!'

Ten minutes later, they were outside, watching with interest as a Panda car driven by PC Bardon, with two young boys in the back, sped past.

'There goes trouble, Ken. I bet those boys know something about the seagulls.'

Madame Volatska sat at her kitchen table with a freshly prepared coffee. She felt cold, despite the heating running flat out. Pulling her bathrobe tightly around herself, she heard the dripping of water behind her. She turned, screamed, and ran to the back door, away from the drenched girl who held out her hands.

Tara Jones made her way upstairs at the Beach View Hotel to prepare the recently vacated room for the next guests. She took the broken lamp and placed it on the trolley and smiled. That smile soon melted away.

When she turned towards the bed to remove the sheets, there lay a young woman, her dark hair about her on the pillow, framing a face so very white, eyes wide open, a trickle of blood upon her right wrist. Tara sank into the chair that stood by the door. She put her hands to her eyes. When she took them away and looked again at the bed, the woman was gone. Tara sat staring, and a terrible feeling of sadness overwhelmed her. She stood up to look out of the window. PC Bardon's Panda car passed along the promenade. It was going to be a busy day for her.

## Chapter 3

Dennis Rawlson had called a colleague at the council and an operation was already in place to clear away the dead seagulls. Townsfolk were now occupying the High Street and watched with equal amounts of interest and disgust as the dead seagulls were loaded into bulging black sacks.

Young mother Debbie Barry pushed the pram containing her precious baby son past a group of council workmen. She paused, intrigued by what had happened. She asked the workman nearest to her what he thought had gone on.

'We have absolutely no idea, love. Horrible, isn't it? Bet it has something to do with local youths.'

Debbie turned and screamed. Her son was out of the pram and lying on the ground surrounded by headless seagulls.

PC Bardon, torch in hand, stood at the rear doors of the Empire Ballroom with Tim Marks and David Rudd. 'Lead the way lads.' He shone his torch through the doorway, confident he would find something that a young boy could mistake for a body but which definitely was not a body.

The boys, David in front, slowed as they approached the bundle he had tripped over just an hour before. He pointed, and PC Bardon swung the beam of his torch downward, illuminating a bearded face, eyes staring upwards.

'Come away, lads. I'm going to need to call this one in on the radio.' He knew whose lifeless body this was. He had in the past had many dealings with this man. It was local vagrant and rough sleeper Frank Chapley. Bardon led the way back with the boys following close behind.

As they reached the door, a man's laughter and then a woman's cry rang out from somewhere within the depths of the ballroom. 'Make your way home, lads. I'm going to have to stay here until reinforcements arrive. Oh, and thanks, but I suggest you stay away from this place in future.'

When the boys arrived home, news of their gruesome find had somehow leaked out and had spread fast as anxious townsfolk passed the word to friends and neighbours.

Dennis Rawlson and Ken Lomes stared at the entrance to the pier. Dennis unlocked the gates and the turnstile. 'Here, Dennis, I've never noticed that before. Bit too late to be introducing a new attraction, isn't it?'

Dennis followed Ken's gaze. 'What on earth!'

There, just beyond the gate, was a red and white striped kiosk with a painted sign: 'Punch and Judy'.

'I assure you I know nothing about that, Ken, but I'm sure I soon will. Come on.'

'I haven't seen a Punch and Judy show on the pier for over forty years, Dennis. It was in that exact place every year when I was a lad.'

As they approached, they stopped. The kiosk, so real seconds before, had gone. All that remained was Mr Punch's maniacal laughter.

'Ken, bring that whisky. I think we're going to need it.'

Madame Volatska, still in just a dressing gown, sat in front of the fire in the back room of the Ship and Anchor while a concerned Julie brought her coffee. 'I'm telling you, Julie, she was definitely there, as real as you are to me now. And she dripped water on my floor. I don't know what to think, but it scared the shit out of me and I'm not someone who scares easily you know, what with my dabbling in the world of spirits. Thank goodness my nephew is coming to stay. I'm not going back there on my own. I'll meet him outside and he can go in first.'

In the High Street, Debbie Barry held her baby son close to her chest as a council worker led her to a bench. The child seemed not the slightest disturbed or injured by whatever had happened, and whatever it was remained a mystery.

By half past eleven, crime scene investigators had completed their work, the body of Frank Chapley was on its way to the mortuary, and PC Bardon had arrived back at the police station to be greeted by a crowd of some twenty people. Among them were three journalists hungry for information about the death and other events in the town that they had become aware of. The rest were members of the public who once inside made reports of the most strange and mysterious nature. By far the most bizarre, reported by two people, was the sighting of an out-of-control car on the seafront that was apparently driverless.

Statements completed, worried residents and business owners placated, PC Bardon locked the door of the police station, ignoring the telephone that had been ringing almost continually since he had arrived earlier. This time he left the Panda car behind and proceeded on foot, his mind in turmoil. By the time he reached the seafront, usually a ten-minute walk, he had been accosted seven, eight, maybe nine times, by concerned townsfolk reporting yet further unusual occurrences and asking questions about the finding of Frank Chapley's body. 'Was violence involved?'

After forty-five minutes, he finally arrived at the commemorative clock tower on the seafront, the affixed plaque there to remind passers-by of a visit to the town by Queen Victoria. Bardon locked down at his wrist-watch then up at one of the faces of the clock, a clock he remembered being told, which had not stopped for over thirty years, to check his own timepiece. The clock had seemingly stopped, its hands frozen at half past one.

Crossing the road, his attention was drawn to the window of the museum. What appeared to be blood had run down the inside surface of the glass. He drew his face close to the pane of glass in the front door, his hands clasped to his cheeks to improve his view. On the white-tiled floor was a symbol: a five-pointed star surrounded by a circle, with a reversed 'Z' at its centre, drawn in what again appeared to be blood, albeit crudely as if scribed by a human finger. Immediate concern for Moira Taggart consumed his thoughts. He had to get to her bungalow now, but that was at least a twenty-minute walk.

He turned, his intention to return to the police station to collect the Panda car. As he did, a small Fiat car hooted and stopped. The driver's window lowered. Behind it was the face of concerned hotel proprietor, Tara Jones.

'PC Bardon. Thank goodness! I was hoping I would see you. I need to tell you something. You'll think I'm losing my mind though!'

The young policeman smiled.

'After some of the things I've heard and seen today, nothing would surprise me, Tara. Anyway, I need to ask you a favour. I left the Panda car back at the police station. Is it possible you could give me a lift to Moira Taggart's place? Something's happened at the museum.'

Tara turned and nodded in the direction of the passenger door of the Fiat. 'Get in, officer!' On the short journey, Tara explained her earlier experience.

The young policeman listened intently, not really knowing how he should reply, but settling for, 'Well, there's a lot of strange things that happened last night. I don't suppose for a minute I've heard the last of them yet.'

Drawing up outside Moira Taggart's bungalow, PC Bardon turned to face Tara. 'Thank you so much, Tara. I owe you.'

The attractive, curvaceous young lady smiled sweetly. 'Oh, that's alright. How could I refuse a handsome man like you. A kiss on the cheek would be payment enough.'

The young policeman blushed, looked around to make sure that no one was watching, and, leaning towards his target, delivered a brief but heartfelt kiss. It was as he drew away that his attention was drawn to the earring that adorned Tara's left lobe. An inverted five-pointed star surrounded by a circle, with a reversed 'Z' at its centre.

## Chapter 4

Inside the Pier Theatre, Dennis and Ken had been playing cards for nearly an hour. In front of Ken was a substantial quantity of money. In front of Dennis, two £1 notes and a two-thirds-empty whisky bottle. Ken picked up the notes in front of him and began sorting them into an orderly pile.

'I think we should call it a day as far as cards are concerned, Dennis.' He took his wallet from his jacket pocket and crammed the notes inside, then struggled to close the now bulging accessory.

Dennis looked up and down and raised his eyebrows. 'One more hand, Ken. At least give me a chance to win some of my money back.'

Ken smiled. 'Maybe a bit later. I need a break.'

Dennis pushed his remaining two £1 notes into his top pocket and proceeded to stack the playing cards in a neat deck. 'Come on then, Ken. Let's go and sit in a couple of the auditorium seats while we finish off what's left of this bottle.

The pair, by then awash with whisky, made their stumbling way to the back row of seats in the theatre auditorium.

Young mother Debbie Barry was back at home still shaken by the events of earlier that day. Undressing her precious son for his bath, she inspected him closely, still not convinced that he had been left unmarked from his apparent fall. Rolling him onto his back, she noticed a small circular red patch on his left shoulder. She looked closer, her brow furrowed, and she screamed. The patch was a symbol: an inverted five-pointed star surrounded by a circle, at its centre a reversed 'Z'.

'PC Bardon, what can I do for you?' Moira Taggart had answered a knock at her front door.

'Moira, apologies for disturbing you. I need to speak to you about the museum. There appears to be some, how shall I put it, damage.'

'Come in, PC Bardon. Let's go through to the front room. I can't take bad news standing up.'

Within a few minutes the young policeman had explained what he saw through the front door window at the museum to Moira, who, in her deep Scottish brogue had some information for him also.

'Last night, two wee lads and their father came to my front door. The lads had been worried because they had seen some flashing lights through the museum window. They were worried it might have been a fire, so they got their father to look. He convinced them it wasn't a fire, but he was concerned. He got my home address from the card in the museum window. They came over and took me down there. I looked around and all seemed in order, or so I told them, as I didn't want to upset the little ones. But something was definitely not alright with one of the displays.

'They've come back for their stuff to protect themselves, you see, and from what you've told me, they'll be needing it.'

PC Bardon's brow furrowed.

Dennis and Ken were still seated in the rear seats at the Pier Theatre. The whisky bottle was empty, and without the distraction of the card game they had begun to discuss and try to rationalise the strange but definite appearance of the Punch and Judy kiosk earlier.

'We both saw it, Dennis, and we were certainly not that worse for wear with drink then. I've heard it's possible for the mind to conjure up images of things we remember.'

Dennis drained the last remaining drops of whisky from his glass. 'That's fine, Ken, but we *both* saw it. I wouldn't remember it anyway. I'd never been here when that was on the pier.'

'Well, that's a spanner in the works of that theory. I reckon we could think clearer if we had another drink. You must still have some stuff behind the theatre bar.'

'I have, Ken, but if I go home pissed at this time of day, Rita will kill me.'

Ken laughed, but his laughter was soon replaced by a gasp and a look of horror. 'Dennis. Look!'

Both men watched transfixed as the stage curtains opened to reveal what appeared to be a body lying prone upon the boards. It took only moments for the two drunken men to stumble their way out of the theatre, although what they encountered outside proved to be an even greater shock.

PC Bardon had walked with Moira Taggart the twenty minutes from her bungalow to the museum. Moira took a sharp intake of breath when she saw the state of the windows. 'I think you'd better open up and take a look. There's something I want to see.'

Unlocking the door and stepping inside, Moira's attention was immediately drawn to the strange symbol on the floor. She sighed.

'Moira, does this symbol mean anything to you?'

For a moment, Moira stood in thought. 'It might, PC Bardon. It might.'

## Chapter 5

Madame Volatska, dressed in little more than a borrowed gentleman's overcoat, had made her way back to her flat, although she was still unwilling to go inside. She lit a cigarette and drew the coat close around her, hoping her nephew would not be much longer. Was it the cold, or was it something else that was making her shiver wildly? Her nephew was only minutes away, fortunately. She placed open palms against her cheeks and pressed her face against the glass of the back door of her flat. On the other side of the glass the white face of a girl with soaking wet hair looked back at her. For a few moments their eyes locked, then the glass misted over, and the silent Madame Volatska, her legs now no firmer than jelly, sank slowly to the floor, which is where her nephew, thirty-year-old publisher's assistant Craig Norton, found her.

Dennis Rawlson and Ken Lomes burst out of the doors of the Pier Theatre, their intention to reach the gates of the pier as quickly as possible. That was before a loud rumbling and splashing sound, followed by a shuddering of the pier structure, made them stop. Their heads turning simultaneously to be met by the sight of a paddle steamer mooring at the pier head.

'Dennis, I don't believe it. It's the *Island Queen*!'

Dennis looked puzzled. 'You recognise her, Ken?'

Ken lowered himself slowly onto one of the nearby benches. 'Recognise her? I saw her two days ago. She's moored in a tributary seven miles away, decaying. She's been there for twenty years that I know of.'

Dennis sank down onto the bench beside Ken. What happened next made them want to get up and continue running.

Madame Volatska's nephew found his aunt lying on the flagstones outside the back door of her flat, dressed in little more than a man's overcoat. Placing his right arm behind her neck, he slowly raised her head. As he did so, his aunt's eyelids fluttered. She was back in the world of the conscious. It would be a few moments more until her eyes focused upon the good-looking young man who stood over her.

'Craig?'

'Mary?'

The exchange of smiles answered that question without the need for words. Craig Norton helped his aunt to her feet.

'It's so good to see you, Craig. Still as handsome as ever!'

She explained all that had happened at her flat during the previous hours, adding, 'I've been waiting for you to arrive before I even think about going in. If I see that girl once more, I swear it will be the end of me.'

Mary handed the keys to her flat to her nephew and took a few steps back as he turned the key in the lock and slowly swung the door open.

'Seems like I've arrived just in time, Mary.'

On the pier Dennis Rawlson and Ken Lomes stood open-mouthed as the long decommissioned paddle steamer *Island Queen* discharged her compliment of strange passengers onto the landing stage. As the last one departed, the years of decay and neglect that the *Island Queen* had suffered reappeared in the space of a minute: paint peeling, windows breaking, superstructure collapsing. Then she was gone, simply fading away. However, the strange passengers remained and were now starting to climb the few steps from the landing stage onto the pier itself.

Dennis and Ken stood as if rooted to the spot as the first of the passengers approached, a man dressed in the style of fifty years before.

He was waving in his hand a small piece of paper in the direction of Dennis Rawlson, while calling out in a raised voice, 'Sir, can you direct us to the Empire Ballroom. There's a gathering there soon, a sort of séance. They're promising some amazing things will happen.' He showed Dennis the paper he held. It was a ticket issued by the Empire Ballroom fifty years previously. On it was a symbol: an inverted five-pointed star surrounded by a circle, with a reversed 'Z' at its centre.

The light of day was beginning to fade, the wind had gathered in strength and a heavy bank of cloud was gathering to the west. Above the Empire Ballroom, a strange blue almost purple glow had begun to form. Outside its doors, a crowd was gathering. Not a crowd of the living, but a crowd of the dead, although to the casual onlooker there would appear to be no difference. But if there was a difference to be observed, it was only in the style of their clothing and the strange distortion of their faces. On the walls on either side of the wide ballroom doors were posters advertising a séance by the Brethren of the Visiting Spirits, and in the centre of the poster, a symbol: an inverted five-pointed star surrounded by a circle, with a reversed 'Z' at its centre. The peculiar, deceased folk of the crowd read and pointed.

## Chapter 6

Publisher's assistant Craig Norton sat at the kitchen table with his aunt, Mary Sharp, better known to the town as Madame Volatska, fortune-teller. Craig had been working for a London publisher, Sebastian and Grosse, who specialised in publishing books on the occult. Following a submission by an author, Ben Greenwood, he had taken time to read a previous book by the same man. In that book, a visit by a society called the Brethren of the Visiting Spirits to Stonypool was described at some length. He had learned that the organisation was set up in 1919 by a man called Simon Clark-Mathos, although it seemed he preferred to be referred to as Master Mathos.

It had started as a small group whose interest was holding séances – fairly innocent and not uncommon at the time – especially with the interest many had in contacting husbands and sons who were victims of the Great War, so recently over. The group had grown rapidly and diversified its interests to include the carrying out of occult practices and rituals. This had led to them being implicated in the deaths of some nine men and women apparently known to the group. The Stonypool gathering was to be their first mass public séance, and their advertising made the bold claim that 'the dead will be raised'. The event took place at Stonypool's Empire Ballroom in late October 1920. The gathering did not go as expected, at least for many of those that attended to see if the dead really were raised. Although maybe the members of the society had expected the night to end in drama, and it most certainly did.

A fire started, which quickly engulfed the ballroom. Forty people lost their lives that night, although none were members of the Brethren of the Visiting Spirits. When interviewed by members of the local press beforehand, Simon Clark-Mathos had said that he believed the town to be a focus of energy that attracted the undead. And he made a wild claim in the form of a curse that would manifest itself in fifty years' time, in Stonypool, when there would be a period of unrest during the day's and night's before when the dead would walk again, re-enacting acts of fifty years of wrongdoing, followed by the release of pure evil This, he said, would last one day for every year the Brethren of the Visiting Spirits continued to exist, which it did for another five years, in one form or another, disbanding when Simon Clark-Mathos disappeared, probably abroad, after being criticised and accused of being a fraud.

Fifty years since that fateful night was soon to pass, and Craig Norton, a man fascinated by all things occult and paranormal, had arrived.

Mary Sharp prepared a coffee for her nephew, pulled the man's overcoat tightly around herself and lit a cigarette.

'It's cold in here, Mary,' said Craig, clasping his hands around his hot mug of coffee.

'It's normally such a warm flat, Craig. Even in the winter it doesn't take much to keep it warm. I have to say it actually makes me feel even more uneasy about being here. Anyway, what brings you all the way from the big city to humble Stonypool? You said something about thinking you'd be needed, I remember.'

Craig sipped his coffee and breathed out, the warmth of his breath visible in vapour as it met the unnatural cold of the room. 'Indeed, I did, Mary, and like I said earlier, I think I've arrived just in time.'

Mary frowned but said nothing.

'The girl you saw, and I certainly don't disbelieve you, you said she was soaking wet?'

'Yes, and she left puddles on my floor. Pale too. I don't even like to conjure her image in my mind.'

Craig pulled his chair closer to the table, leaned forward and stared fixedly into his aunt's eyes. 'Mary, you have an open mind. You have to, doing what you do, I mean, the fortune-telling. You know of course the girl is a ghost, don't you?'

Mary laughed, causing her to inhale an unexpectedly large lungful of cigarette smoke.

'Of course I know. Believe me, if it had been a living girl, she would have been out that door in seconds!'

Craig relaxed. At least that hurdle was passed.

'Before I explain what brought me down here, Mary, tell me, are you aware of any other, shall we say, less than ordinary happenings in the town?'

'Well, they told me at the pub that nearly all the glasses in the saloon bar were smashed overnight. Oh, and someone at the Ship and Anchor had said something about the pavement in the High Street being littered with the bodies of dead headless seagulls this morning. *And* there was that vagrant found dead. Unusual occurrence for Stonypool, but it happens to those poor buggers sometimes.'

Craig sat in thought for a moment.

'A death you say? A vagrant. Where was the body found, Mary?'

'Inside the old Empire Ballroom. Kids found him. Obviously went in there for shelter. Old Frank Chapley it was. Well known in the town. Harmless fellow. Is it significant where he was found, I mean, in the old ballroom?'

'It could well be, Mary. Tell me, have you ever heard of a society called the Brethren of the Visiting Spirits? They existed fifty years ago.'

Mary shook her head. 'I can't say I have, Craig.'

Leaning sideways from his chair, Craig unzipped the bag in which he had packed sufficient changes of clothes for a five-day stay, and he took out a paperback book, which he placed on the table in front of Mary. He opened it at a page marked by a makeshift bookmark. On the page were the words: 'The Brethren of the Visiting Spirits and the Stonypool Séance'. Below was a symbol: an inverted five-pointed star surrounded by a circle, with a reversed 'Z' at its centre.

An hour later Mary Sharp knew much about the Brethren of the Visiting Spirits.


## Chapter 7

Above the Empire Ballroom the blue almost purple light had grown more intense, or maybe it just seemed that way against the darkening skies and storm clouds. Storm clouds that within a few minutes would release a torrential downpour, accompanied by lightning that made the air crackle. But of course, the gathered crowd outside didn't care. After all, they were just a strange visage of those dead people who had come to watch a séance performed almost fifty years before. The strange crowd, satisfied that the séance they wished to attend was indeed to be held on the day advertised, dispersed into the town, leaving the pavement outside the old Empire Ballroom empty.

Dennis Rawlson and Ken Lomes had wasted no time in returning to the relative comfort of the Ship and Anchor, where of course another few whiskies were quickly imbibed by the still speechless pair.

Julie, the new barmaid, was keen to speak to Ken, beckoning him to the bar. 'We've had some right weirdos in here tonight, complaining bitterly that we were blatantly ripping them off with our prices. Martin Dawes down at the arcade reckons he'd had them in there too. Showed them the door, he did. He reckons that one of them said something about a séance at the Empire Ballroom of all things! Isn't that where people try to communicate with the dead? That sort of thing gives me the creeps.'

PC Bardon had helped Moira Taggart to tidy the museum following a visit by the scenes of crime team who had really found very little to account for what had happened. No signs of forced entry, no fingerprints, and, not unexpectedly, nothing to account for the strange lights. They had spent some considerable time looking at the strange symbol drawn upon the floor and it was decided that it was the same substance as had run down the inside of the windows. That substance was now drying into a dark reddish-brown coating. They had agreed that it was blood. Its source was found in the cobbled rear yard, where the remains of a small animal, almost certainly a fox, lay in a heap of grotesque blood and gore. As for the symbol, all present, except one, declared that they had never seen it before. That one was Moira Taggart.

'I've seen it before. Many years ago. There was a society that did bad things, tried to raise the dead. When I first moved down here, there was a story circulating of how they had visited the town and that whatever it was that they did in the Empire Ballroom ended badly. I can't think now what they were called, as it was years ago. Why on earth would anyone want to drag all that up again? I remember that symbol. It was on a flier for the event that I had as an exhibit in the museum when we first opened. If I knew where it was, I would show you.'

As PC Bardon walked away from the museum, a memory came to him that, for a moment, stopped him in his tracks. He had seen that symbol before, at least he thought he had, in Tara Jones' car. Her earring. Looking towards the old Empire Ballroom and seeing the strange lights, he wasn't sure what the coming night would hold for the town, but he was sure it was unlikely to be good.

There was a flash of lightning and a rumble of thunder. The rain began to fall upon Stonypool once again.

## Chapter 8

### Day Three

Mary Sharp had slept surprisingly well, helped by the reassurance that her nephew was asleep in the room next to hers. He was indeed in that room, but sleep had largely evaded him after, a girl in a white dress with dark hair, and thoroughly soaked, at midnight, had loomed over him, dripping freezing cold water onto his face and bedclothes.

Dennis Rawlson hadn't made it home, having passed out in a back room of the Ship and Anchor. After the drinking of the previous day, he had awoken with a dry mouth and a thumping headache, memories of the strange events of the previous twenty-hours coming back to him. Did all that really happen?

Rita Rawlson had waited for her husband to return. She needed to vent the fury that had built up within her during the day. But by the early hours of the morning, she had locked the doors and retired to bed, her anger making sleep slow in coming. But when it did, she dreamt that her husband was in bed with her and between them, tight against her, was another person. In that dream, she switched on the bedside light, raised herself and looked into a face she knew well: her own. The right arm of her doppelgänger lay above the bedclothes, and clasped in its hand was a bloodied knife. Her husband lay still, his eyes wide open, his throat cut. She had awoken with a start.

The dream had not shocked her, only compounded the hate she felt for her wayward husband. The rest of the night she had struggled to sleep but had eventually succumbed. Waking at half past nine, she turned over in bed to look at where her husband should have been. Although his space was empty, she was relieved that he wasn't lying motionless, staring, and with his throat cut.

The anger boiled within her. She knew where he would have spent the night: with bloody Ken Lomes at the Ship and Anchor. She turned over and picked up the receiver of the telephone that sat upon her bedside cabinet. There was no dial tone. With the middle finger of her left hand, she clicked the buttons on the receiver cradle.

Through the wires and into Rita's ears came a voice: dark, deep and menacing.

'Kill Dennis!'


At the police station the telephone on the front desk was ringing as PC Bardon unlocked the door. Hanging his coat up on the public side of the desk, he picked up the receiver.

'Stonypool Police Station. PC Bardon speaking.'

'It's Richard Ryan at the mortuary here. I have something most irregular to report. The body of that vagrant that was brought in yesterday, Frank Chapley, it's gone!'

Bardon paused briefly before replying, 'Let me get this right, the body of the vagrant that was brought to you yesterday is gone? Any sign of forced entry or anything else unusual?'

'No. I was the first to arrive this morning and the building was locked – just as I had left it late yesterday. No windows were open or broken. I really don't understand it. Just one thing though, the head of the cadaver on the slab next to where Chapley's body had been laid had been uncovered, and on the forehead a symbol had been cut. It's an inverted five-pointed star surrounded by a circle, with a reversed 'Z' at the centre.'

Grabbing his coat from the hook upon which he had placed it only moments before, Bardon, in a firm voice told Richard Ryan to 'stay put' adding, 'I'll be there within ten minutes.'

As he clicked the front door behind him, the telephone rang again, only this time it was picked up by the answering machine:

'This is Stonypool Police Station. I'm sorry we can't answer your call at the moment, but please leave a message after the tone. If your call is an emergency, please replace your handset and dial 999.'

'Hello. This is Tara Jones at the Beach View Hotel calling for PC Bardon. You're not going to believe this ... Frank Chapley just tried to check in! Call me back when you get this message.'

That was to be another two hours away.

Elsewhere in town, another telephone was ringing, this one at the Ship and Anchor. It too was picked up by an answering machine;

'Hello, this is Ken Lomes at the Ship and Anchor. I can't get to the telephone right now. Please leave a message after the tone.'

'Hello Ken. It's Rita Rawlson. I know Dennis is with you. Send him straight home when you get this. I have a surprise for him.'

Ken didn't need to pass on the message; Dennis had heard it while making his way to the gents for the fifth time that morning. Two aspirin tablets and four cups of coffee later, he left the comforts of the Ship and Anchor and headed towards home. After all, Rita didn't sound angry on the telephone and she had a surprise for him, didn't she?

PC Bardon arrived back at the police station after his visit to the mortuary. Frank Chapley's body had indeed disappeared. Not that he had doubted the word of Richard Ryan for a moment. But it's not often, maybe never, that a policeman is presented with a missing body, especially one which appears to have been taken from a locked building with no sign of forced entry.

It had been an hour before Richard Ryan's assistant had thought to check the small key safe where the spare keys for the mortuary were kept. Those keys weren't there, but that in itself only compounded the mystery. A corpse, rising from the slab, finding the keys, unlocking the door to let itself out, and then taking the trouble to lock the door behind it before walking into the night … what are the chances of that?

Preparing himself a strong coffee, PC Bardon clicked the button on the station's answering machine and, listening to Tara Jones' message, decided to add an extra teaspoonful of instant coffee to his mug. Today, he was going to need all his wits about him.

Rita Rawlson had been waiting an hour for her husband to return since her telephone call to the Ship and Anchor. It was only a five-minute walk. What was taking him so long? In the first ten minutes of that hour, she had selected her sexiest lingerie, sprayed her body with her sweetest and most expensive perfume, and to complete her husband's surprise, had taken something from a drawer in the kitchen. She looked at her watch: an hour and ten minutes. Now her anger was starting to boil, but she knew she must turn down the heat. She needed to appear demure, provocative, sexy.

She heard his key in the door, then his footsteps in the hallway. She called out, 'Dennis, darling, I'm up here. I have a surprise for you.'

The hapless husband threw his coat to the floor and bounded up the stairs, where he found his wife looking quite presentable, especially, he thought to himself, as he hadn't had a drink that morning.

'Dennis, darling, I've been waiting for you for ages.'

With that, Rita Rawlson beckoned with a finger, pulled back the bedclothes and then slipped between the sheets.

Hungover as he was, Dennis was not going to turn down this opportunity, on two counts: the first being that his wife was in a good mood, which was rare; and that she was clearly offering him sex, something that had not even been hinted at for months. Stripping off his shirt and trousers, he heaved his body onto the bed beside his wife, whose nostrils were immediately assaulted by the smell of his unwashed body and his foetid breath.

It was all she could do not to gag, let alone smile sweetly at the mess of a man who was her husband. *Not for much longer,* she thought, which helped her maintain that smile as Dennis rolled towards her and raised his head with the clear intention of planting a kiss on her lips. Rita drew up her right arm and from under the covers withdrew a long kitchen knife, that in a second was against her husband's throat.

'Rita. What the – '

Dennis slipped from the bed, ran across to the French doors, which opened onto the small balcony and which fortunately were unlocked. And wearing just his underpants, he jumped into the street below, landing heavily. As he lay there winded and with his right leg at a peculiar angle underneath him, he called out to a figure wrapped in a white sheet who was coming slowly towards him, 'Help me, please. Help me. My wife is trying to kill me.'

Frank Chapley stopped, looked down at him, and laughed.

## Chapter 9

'I didn't have a great night, Mary.'

Craig Norton appeared in the kitchen of Mary Sharp's flat, dark semi-circles under his eyes, his hair somewhat dishevelled. 'She appeared. That girl. It wasn't that she frightened me, I just felt so sorry for her. The cold water in the early hours wasn't very pleasant either. How did you sleep?'

Mary smiled at him as she lit her third cigarette that morning.

'Much better knowing you were just next door, my darling.'

Her nephew waved his hand to deflect the cloud of pungent cigarette smoke that was headed in his direction.

'Mary, do you know if it's possible still to get access to the Empire Ballroom? I know it's been closed for a long time, but I really think it's central to what is happening in the town.'

Mary flicked an inch of ash from her cigarette with one hand while fiddling with the packet with the other.

'I wouldn't have thought so, at least not legally. Since that vagrant died in there, even the potentially legal routes have been nailed up solid. Dennis Rawlson might know. He's the manager of the pier and lives locally. He knows a lot of influential people. He's on the council, too. You could maybe arrange to meet him there?'

That meeting wasn't to happen – at least not that day.

Dennis Rawlson was on his way to hospital, his wife by his side – although he couldn't bear to look at her.

By eleven o'clock, Craig Norton had breakfasted and consumed a cup of strong coffee in Seashells Cafe. It had been quiet and he had got chatting with Tony Gorse, the proprietor, who opened the conversation.

'So, what do you reckon about all the strange shit that's been happening around here lately? Those dead seagulls didn't do much for trade in the High Street, I can tell you. And what about the influx of weirdos yesterday? Had a couple of them in here, asking if I could hand out fliers for some peculiar event. I told them to fuck off.'

'Yeah, I was chatting to some people on the way here. They told me about some of that strange stuff. Didn't get hold of one of those fliers, I suppose?'

'No. I started to read one and when I realised it was weird shit, I gave it back.'

Craig leaned sideways and fumbled in the rucksack that he had put by his chair. He took out a book, placed it on the table and opened it at a page he had bookmarked, then turned it round to face Tony.

'Didn't have a symbol like this on it, did it?'

'Yeah. That's it. Like I said, weird shit. And it's in a book. *Famous* weird shit! What is it anyway?'

Craig rotated the book and stared intently at the printed symbol. 'It's the symbol of a society that hasn't been around for fifty odd years. They used to claim they could raise the dead.'

Tony looked amused.

'That might explain what happened to Tara Jones at the Beach View Hotel this morning then?'

Craig raised his head and looked inquiringly at his new breakfast companion.

'What exactly did happen at the hotel, Tony?'

Tony Gorse leaned forward, put a finger against his lips and spoke in a hushed voice. 'Called me this morning she did. Asked if I could drop a loaf of bread over to her. Said she couldn't get to the shop. Said she was waiting for the police to call. Reckons she's had a dead guy wanted to check in. What do you make of that? She's of a mind that it was that old vagrant, Frank Chapley, the one those kids found dead in the Empire Ballroom. No clothes on either, just a white sheet wrapped around him. I didn't really ly know what to think. I hear Tara sometimes likes an early gin if the place is quiet.'

Craig Norton closed the book and put it back in his bag. 'Tell me, do you know where I might find Dennis Rawlson?'

'Yeah, right now most likely the hospital. Apparently, he fell from his balcony at home this morning. Broke his leg, they reckon. Probably trying to get away from that awful wife of his, Rita. Rita the Cheater, I call her.'

'Look thanks, er ...?'

'Tony. Tony Gorse. Most people call me Big Tony. It's certainly not on account of my stature. Mind you, seems to be only the ladies that call me that!' Tony gave Craig an over-exaggerated wink.

'I'm Craig Norton. I expect you've heard of Madame Volatska, the fortune-teller? I'm her nephew.'

Tony smiled. 'Yeah, you mean Mary Sharp. Lovely lady. Comes in here regularly. I keep telling her to lay off the fags. Here, have a word with her about it, will you?'

Standing to leave, Craig held out a hand to Tony. 'Thanks, Tony. You've been a great help. If you fancy a pint tonight, I'm buying. Where's a good pub?'

Tony shook Craig's hand firmly. 'Ship and Anchor, just along the front. Don't mind if I do, buddy. See you later.'

# Chapter 10

PC Bardon had been at the Beach View Hotel for half an hour. He had taken a short statement from Tara Jones, who was now sitting uncomfortably close to him on a sofa in the hotel television room, the young policeman's attention somewhat distracted by the ample cleavage on display. 'Tara, as there's actually been no crime committed, your statement will be filed alongside the others that have been given in relation to the unusual events in the town. There is something I'd like to ask you though.'

Tara smiled, flashing her even white teeth. 'The answer is yes, PC Bardon! I would love to have a drink with you.'

The young constable flushed with embarrassment. 'Erm, no Tara. Though of course ... No, it's about those earrings you were wearing today when you gave me a lift up to Moira Taggart's place.'

Tara feigned a look of disappointment. 'You can't blame a girl for trying.' She gently stroked the back of her left hand with a perfectly manicured finger.

'Yes, about the earrings, Tara.'

'My earrings? What about my earrings?'

'Is it possible I could see them?'

'PC Bardon, you'll be asking to see my underwear next!'

Although now a little impatient, the young constable could not suppress a smile.

Tara bit her lip and shook her hair seductively. 'Now, what possible interest could the law have in my earrings? If you want to come upstairs, I'll show you them.'

'Er ... maybe not, Tara. Probably best if you fetch them and bring them downstairs.'

Tara giggled. 'Whatever you say, handsome. Be back in a moment.'

Five minutes passed. Bardon looked at his watch, at which moment Tara sprang back into the room. Was that the same skirt she had left the room wearing? It seemed so much shorter, the embarrassed young constable thought. In her right hand she held a small velvet box, which she handed to him.

'These are the ones.'

Bardon opened the box. They were indeed the ones. Gold, around three quarters of an inch across, an inverted five-pointed star surrounded by a circle, with a reversed 'Z' at the centre. 'Tara, tell me, how did you come to own these?'

Tara looked confused. 'They're not stolen if that's what you're hinting at?'

Bardon clicked the little box closed. 'No, it's nothing like that. You for one are well aware of all the strange things that have been happening in the town over the last couple of days. Well, the symbol represented by these earrings has been associated with some of those events.'

Tara lowered the hem of her skirt and sat down again, even closer to the young policeman, who, looking down decided that it was not the same skirt. 'They were my grandmother's. She gave them to me a few months before she died. She was a member of a peculiar society in her earlier days and the symbol on those earrings was theirs. My parents refused to talk about her involvement, but occasionally she would tell me a little of what they had been involved with. Although I have to say that I was not at all comfortable with it.

'Seems they met in groups in an attempt to raise the spirits of the dead. And the ultimate aim was to raise the dead themselves. She left my grandfather and went to live with the Master of the society. I don't know whether she was romantically involved with him, but from the way she spoke about him I'm pretty sure she had been.

'After a few years the society broke up and he disappeared. She came back to the family with her tail between her legs, although things were never the same. It seems whatever had happened to her while under his influence had affected her mind. She still performed peculiar rituals that I remember well from my childhood.

'When she died, she had no money. She had apparently given all her savings to the society. The few worldly possessions she had were passed down to me: a few items of cheap jewellery and a wooden chest with that same symbol on the lid. It had apparently belonged to the Master, and she had told me before she died that it contained items that could be used in the summoning of the dead. I've never opened it. It gives me the creeps.'

PC Bardon had listened attentively. 'Thanks, Tara, you've been most, how shall I say, enlightening. Although the connection between that symbol and what has been happening confounds me.'

Bardon raised himself from the sofa, closed his notebook and prepared to leave as Tara added:

'There's something I forgot to tell you that may help to make some sense of this. My grandmother told me the society once came to Stonypool on what she called their "Tours". They held what I suppose you could describe as a séance at the Empire Ballroom. It didn't end well. There was a fire. All the members of the society who were there escaped unharmed, but a great many of the audience perished. It's a strange thing. She told me that she was pleased she would not be around to see if the Master's curse came true. Despite me asking, she never did tell me what she meant.'

## Chapter 11

Craig Norton stood outside the front of the old Empire Ballroom. He had walked all around the outside of the looming, decaying structure, but, as his aunt had suspected, every possible entry point – bar the locked front doors – had been boarded over and warning notices advising of security patrols glued to those boards.

Stepping closer to the filthy glass doors that opened into the foyer of the building, he clasped his hands to the sides of his face and peered through the cleanest area of one of them. He reeled back in shock as a face on the inside met his. Then came the sound of a key chain rattling against the glass and keys being turned in locks.

The door swung inwards and he was greeted by a man he guessed to be in his fifties, wearing a brown warehouse coat and holding a torch, who smiled broadly.

'Good morning. Can I help you?'

In his surprised state, Craig Norton was momentarily stuck for words. 'Well, er ... I was just interested by the place. Sorry.'

The man's smile became even broader. 'Interested? A grand old building, isn't she? Well, come in and I'll show you around. Not at her best at the moment, I have to say. I'm Vic Gaskill by the way. I sort of look after the place.'

Craig immediately felt at ease. 'Craig Norton. I really didn't expect to find anyone here.'

'No, well you wouldn't normally. Only it's a bit of a special time, you see. Anyway, let me lock the door again, and then follow me.'

The only light in the foyer came from what little daylight could penetrate the filth-encrusted glass in the front doors.

'A bit dark in this part. There's lights in the ballroom itself. Still got electricity. Not sure who pays the bill, but that's none of my concern.'

Through a pair of heavy double doors, they entered the ballroom. Craig's unexpected tour guide flicked a switch, which was located behind a small cover on a wall just inside. There was a buzzing sound, and around the balcony, at first dim but rapidly becoming brighter, lights began to illuminate the scene.

'Like I said, it's suffered from a great deal of neglect in recent times.'

Craig let his eyes scan from left to right. Yes, neglect was most apparent, as was furniture and equipment left behind from the building's last use as a bingo hall. In the beams of the bright lights, dust floated in almost stationary suspension, the air being so still, and when breathed in through the nose, stagnant. Despite the lack of care and attention, Craig was taken aback by the sheer size and beauty of the space where many years before people had come to dance, laugh and maybe find romance.

Vic Gaskill took a few steps forward.

'Follow me. I'll show you the stage. Mind where you're walking though, there's some pretty big holes in the floor here and there.'

Vic led the way, Craig following close behind, his eyes upward looking from left to right. Vic's urgent call focused his attention. 'Look out! Big hole coming up!'

Craig stopped and looked down and slightly ahead. Some ten feet ahead was a hole around six feet wide and eight feet long. He stepped to his right to allow himself to pass well clear of it. His guide kept on walking, passing over the hole as if it were solid floor. A shiver ran down Craig's spine.

'Round to the right now. We go through that door and then climb a few steps to our right and we'll be on the stage.'

Craig followed somewhat less willingly now. They passed through the doorway and Vic flicked another switch, illuminating the small passageway and the few steps that led up to the stage. It now occurred to Craig that although his own footsteps upon the wooden floors created a hollow echo, those of his guide didn't.

'See that big square in the middle of the stage? That was where the organ would rise up. I'm told it's still down there. I'm going to take a look one of these days.'

They crossed the stage and descended an identical set of wooden steps to those on the other side. Rather than turning right, which would have taken them back to the ballroom itself, Vic led the way to the left along a dark passageway, which after around twenty feet opened out into a large room. A hint of daylight could be seen around what were obviously doors ahead of them. There was the sound of another switch being flicked, and the area was dimly illuminated by a single, shadeless bulb that hung from the centre of the ceiling. Craig looked about himself. Just a few feet in front of him, there was a length of discarded polythene tape bearing the repeating legend: 'POLICE LINE. DO NOT CROSS'.

He turned to face Vic. 'I suppose this is where those kids found the body of that old man. Must have been quite a shock for them.'

Vic's face took on an expression of confusion. 'What old man was that then?'

Craig said no more on the matter, rapidly changing the subject.

'Tell me, Vic. Do you know anything about a fire that happened here many years ago?'

Vic took a few moments to answer. 'The big one or the little one? Nobody died in the little one if that helps.'

'The big one then?'

'Funny old business that one. There was what I suppose you could call "a gathering" by a strange society. Can't think what they were called now.'

'The Brethren of the Visiting Spirits?'

'Yes, that's the one. Reckoned they could contact the spirit world, maybe even raise the dead. A fire started in the roof. It wasn't noticed until it was too late, and tons of burning timber and fittings fell onto the audience. Here, follow me, I'll show you something.'

He led the way back down the dark passage out into the light of the ballroom and then round to some stairs, comprising three flights, that ascended to the balcony. They stood in the light of one of the powerful lamps fitted above them. 'Over here.' Vic had walked a few feet further on and called for Craig to follow him. He was pointing to an area of sloping wall at the back of the balcony where a large area of decorative panelling had fallen away and was hanging down like a flap. 'If you look at the woodwork behind where the panel was, you can still see where the wood is charred. The edges of the roof survived. Just.'

The sound of a voice from the ballroom below made Craig turn to look over the edge of the balcony.

'What was that, Vic? Has somebody else followed us in here?' There was no answer. 'Vic?' Turning, Craig realised that his guide was no longer nearby. No sign of him anywhere on the balcony. A moment later, all lighting in the ballroom extinguished and that one voice was joined by many others which all began to accompany each other in a melodious chant that grew louder and louder.

## Chapter 12

Ken Lomes sat by Dennis Rawlson's hospital bed. Dennis had sent his wife home and had instructed the hospital staff that she was to be kept away from him. 'I tell you Ken, it was bloody frightening. I always knew she had a temper, but this? They reckon I might be discharged tomorrow. I can't go home, can I? Not after this.'

Ken put another of the grapes Rita had brought for Dennis in his mouth and sat in thought while he chewed it. 'Well, you're always welcome at the pub, Dennis. I'll get the dining room out the back cleared for you and bring a bed down from upstairs.'

They were joined by a young nurse. 'Mr Rawlson, the doctor has agreed that you can be discharged tomorrow, as long as you have someone at home to look after you. It's going to be at least six weeks until you'll be rid of that cast. Oh, and there's a Constable Bardon here to see you.'

PC Bardon pulled up a chair and sat next to the bed.

'Good afternoon, Dennis. So sorry about your accident. Of course, this wouldn't normally be a police matter, but your wife came to see me. She was very concerned that you might approach the police. Can you tell me what happened from your perspective.'

Dennis looked towards Ken, who said nothing but shook his head.

'It was an argument. My fault. I had been out all night and Rita was really mad. And to be honest, I don't blame her. She was in the bedroom when I got home. The argument escalated and after some pushing and shoving, we ended up on the balcony. Somehow, I toppled over the edge and now here I am.'

Bardon looked up from his notebook.

'Thanks, Dennis. That's essentially what your wife said. I don't think we need to take the matter any further.' The young policeman rose from his chair.

Ken rose also and shook his hand.

'Don't worry, PC Bardon. I'll be looking after him for a few days just in case things kick off again, you know, let the dust settle.' Sitting back down, he took another grape from the rapidly diminishing bunch.

'You did the right thing, Dennis. If you told them what really happened, Rita would be charged with attempted murder. We need to work out where you go from here though. I mean, with your marriage.'

Rita Rawlson sat at her kitchen table, a glass of vodka and tonic in her right hand. The letterbox rattled. She put down her glass and made her way to the front door. On the mat was a sheet of folded paper. Stooping down to pick it up, she unfolded it, her brow furrowing as she read the words: 'You failed. Try again.'

It wasn't so much the words that caused her to frown, but the strange symbol printed at the head of the paper: an inverted five-pointed star surrounded by a circle, with a reversed 'Z' at its centre.

Craig Norton stood alone on the balcony of the Empire Ballroom. The sudden loss of the bright lights to which he had become accustomed left his vision badly impaired. Below him the chanting had become louder, reverberating around the vast ballroom. Looking over the balcony revealed little. Then came a rumble, then another and another, gaining in volume. *Thunder?* thought Craig. *Surely that can't be thunder?* After all, the weather had been clear and settled when he had entered the building not twenty minutes before. Then it came again, but now much louder.

The balcony on which he stood shook, the movement enough to loosen wood and plaster that fell around and onto him. He gripped the rail around the edge as the chanting became louder still, as loud as the near continuous rumbling of what really did sound like thunder. Then, gradually, the ballroom became illuminated by blue almost purple light.

Peering over the edge of the balcony, upturned faces locked upward, forty maybe fifty. Only those faces weren't illuminated by that blueish purple light but by flickering orange light, as if they were looking into a great and fierce fire. The chanting stopped and was replaced by screams and shouting. Then the ballroom fell silent.

The darkness returned, only not entirely. A faint blue almost purple glow remained. Looking above him, in that strange light, as if projected from below onto the ceiling of the ballroom, some twenty feet above was a symbol maybe fifteen feet across: an inverted five-pointed star surrounded by a circle, with a reversed 'Z' at its centre, which was slowly fading.

In what little light remained, and working from recent memory, Craig retraced his steps along the balcony, tripping and stumbling over hazards that had not been there ten minutes before. He located the steps and made his way falteringly to the ballroom below, and then through the door by the stage which opened onto the narrow passage that led to the back room where Frank Chapley's body had been found the day before. Using the small amount of daylight that showed around the frame, Craig located the rear doors, which to his relief he found unlocked, albeit boarded by plywood nailed roughly to the frame, which with three firm kicks fell to the ground outside, allowing daylight to flood in. For just a few moments, he stood outside the doorway inhaling lungfuls of the fresh invigorating air before walking along the side of the ballroom and around to the front entrance where he stood and looked up at the blue cloudless sky.

From across the road came a shout. 'Over here. Come and give me a hand.'

PC Bardon stood looking over the low seawall. Muffled cries for help were coming up to him from below. In a few seconds Craig was by the constable's side.

'What's happened?'

'Look over the wall.'

Looking over, Craig saw an old man suspended by some protruding steel work by the tails of his overcoat that had been pulled up above his head about six feet below. Although he knew it was wrong, Craig couldn't help but smile. 'How did he end up down there?'

'I don't know, but we're soon going to find out. Follow me.'

PC Bardon led the way to a flight of wooden steps that passed through a gap in the seawall from the promenade to the beach. The man was suspended, with his feet around eighteen inches from the sand below. Bardon assessed the situation. 'Keep calm, sir. We're going to lift you by your legs and unhook you. Keep your weight pressed firmly against the seawall, and whatever you do, don't lean forward.'

Taking a leg each, Craig Norton and PC Bardon pushed the relatively light frame of the old man upwards until they judged that he was unhooked from the protruding steelwork, then slowly they allowed him to slide down the seawall until he stood on his feet on the beach.

'Thank you, constable, and you, young man.'

'You're lucky I was passing, Mr, er ...?'

'Booth. Ron Booth.'

'Well, Mr Booth, however did you end up suspended by your overcoat on the seawall?' The smile came back to Craig Norton's face, but he turned away until he could stifle it.

'You're not going to believe this, constable, but I was walking along minding my own business when what I thought was a ghost came towards me from the opposite direction, and all I could think to do was to leap over the seawall.'

'A ghost, Mr Booth?'

'Yes. I know you're going to find this hard to believe, but whatever it was, it was the height of a man but covered almost completely in a white sheet.'

PC Bardon most certainly did believe it. Another sighting of dead vagrant Frank Chapley, he presumed.

Ron Booth made his way somewhat unsteadily from the beach.

Craig laughed. 'Let's hope he doesn't see another ghost, officer.'

48

'That's not as crazy as it may sound Mr ...?'

'Norton. Craig Norton. You probably know of my aunt, Madame Volatska?'

'Ah, yes, Mary. Mary Sharp.'

Craig smiled and held out his hand. 'Well, unusual circumstances, but it's good to meet you, officer. I don't find it crazy in the slightest. In fact, it's exactly what brings me down here. Now you'll think that *I'm* crazy. You probably don't know, but the disturbed period in this town was predicted fifty years ago.'

PC Bardon made his way back towards the wooden steps that led back up to the promenade, with Craig Norton following close behind.

'A few days ago, Mr Norton, I would definitely have considered you a little crazy, but considering all that's happened around here recently, I'm not so sure. You say it's what brought you down here?'

They had reached the top of the steps.

'Indeed. Tell me, have you ever heard of a society now long disbanded called the Brethren of the Visiting Spirits?'

PC Bardon took out his notebook and began to write.

'Tell me, Mr Norton, Craig, would this organisation have used the symbol of an inverted five-pointed star surrounded by a circle, with a reversed 'Z' at its centre. Something like this?' Bardon showed Craig a small sketch on a page of his notebook.

'Yes, that's it. That was their symbol. You've seen it before then?'

'Seen it, Craig? More times in less than two days than you would believe. I'd be very interested to hear more about this, but here is really not the place. Maybe you could call in and see me at the police station later. After five should be fine, providing no more strange stuff requires my attention. Thanks for your help by the way. See you later hopefully.'

Bardon turned and began to walk away to the west along the promenade. He stopped and turned around to face Craig Norton again. 'Craig, you might want to speak to Tara Jones at the Beach View Hotel.'

# Chapter 13

Young mother Debbie Barry sat in an armchair in her living room, watching an early afternoon film on the television, having settled her son for his afternoon sleep in his nursery upstairs. She switched on the baby monitor and sipped her well deserved mug of coffee. Fifteen minutes into the film she had begun to doze, when she was brought sharply back to reality by what sounded like laughter from the speaker of the baby monitor on the table beside her. For a few seconds she thought she had fallen asleep and that it was just one of those strange things sometimes experienced when a person drifts between the worlds of the conscious and the unconscious. But then it came again: maniacal laughter. Then a man's voice:

'We need him. A new life for an old life. We must take him.'

A woman's cackling laughter followed.

Debbie leapt from her chair, sending her half-empty coffee mug flying, bounded up the stairs, and burst into the nursery. Her heart beating rapidly, she looked over the edge of the cot. Her precious son was not there. And scratched into the paintwork at the head of his cot was a symbol: an inverted five-pointed star surrounded by a circle, with a reversed 'Z' at its centre.

Craig Norton stood at the reception desk of the Beach View Hotel and rang the small bell with a stroke of his right hand. A few seconds later Tara Jones appeared behind the desk, flicking her hair and pulling her top down to reveal even more cleavage.

'Good morning, sir. Is it a room you're after?' Craig Norton felt a little flustered.

'Er, well, not exactly. Are you Tara Jones?'

'I am, and who might be asking? Not that I mind being asked by a handsome young man.' Craig felt himself blushing.

'My name is Craig. Craig Norton. You would almost certainly have heard of my aunt, Madame Volatska? I'm in town because of the strange things that have been happening around here over the last couple of days. I met a PC Bardon earlier and he suggested I should talk to you. I'm not sure why?'

Tara smiled. Craig's heart beat faster.

'The lovely PC Bardon. Oh yes. I think I scare him, though I'm not sure why. Madame Volatska, Mary Sharp. Yes, I know Mary very well. Lovely lady. Needs to give up smoking though. She's never mentioned having a handsome nephew. So, what has PC Bardon said?'

'Well, nothing detailed really, but he obviously thought you could help me regarding the strange things that have been happening.'

Tara lifted the flap in the reception desk.

'Come through to the back and I'll show you what I've got. I mean, tell you what I know, and show you ... Oh damn it! This way.' She beckoned to her handsome young visitor to sit down on a sofa. 'Hold on there a minute.'

She left the room by a door to the right of the sofa and in a moment returned holding a small velvet box. Sitting close beside Craig, she opened the box and handed it to him. 'Well, it was these that really sparked PC Bardon's interest. He noticed them yesterday when I gave him a lift. He'd seen the symbol before at some of the places where weird things had happened. He wanted to know where I had got them from, so I explained that my grandmother had been a member of a society many years ago and that's where they had come from. She gave them to me.'

Craig studied the contents of the little velvet box.

'The Brethren of the Visiting Spirits.'

Tara's brow furrowed. 'Who?'

'The society that used this symbol, the Brethren of the Visiting Spirits.'

Tara smiled and shuffled a little closer to Craig.

'Oh yes. I remember now. I've been trying to think what they were called since PC Bardon visited. Those aren't the only things I've got with that symbol on.'

She rose from the sofa, taking Craig's left hand in her right as she did so. 'Come upstairs with me. I'll show you something.' Craig's heart was beating so fast it was almost in his throat as Tara led the way upstairs.

'Tell me, Tara, has anything strange happened here over the last couple of days?'

'Well, if a dead woman in a bed who simply vanished, and a dead man – a man I knew at that – trying to check in isn't strange, then I don't know what is. He was the man those kids found – Frank Chapley – dead at the old Empire Ballroom. That's why I called PC Bardon.' Tara led Craig Norton to her bedroom. 'Let me show you my chest.' By now, it was all Craig could do to suppress his laughter. 'Or more correctly, my *grandmother's* chest.'

He wasn't sure whether he was relieved or disappointed. Tara removed a throw from an object in the corner of her bedroom. Underneath was a wooden chest around eighteen inches tall, twenty-four inches wide and eighteen inches deep. Its most significant feature, the symbol of the Brethren of the Visiting Spirits, was carved into the lid and inlaid with brass.

'What's inside, Tara?'

Tara took a step backwards as if she didn't want to get too close to the box.

'I don't know. I've never opened it. My grandmother always told me that it contained items for raising the dead. She was given it by the Master of that weird society. You see, I think she had an affair with him. Caused huge problems within the family.'

Craig nodded and stooped to run a finger around the engraved symbol, and said, 'Simon Clark-Mathos.'

'Who?' Tara frowned.

'Simon Clark-Mathos. Master Mathos he liked to be called. It was him who formed the Brethren of the Visiting Spirits.'

Tara sat on her bed.

'I never knew his name. We were forbidden to discuss the matter at home. I normally keep that chest in a spare room, I only brought it in here as an excuse to get PC Bardon up to my bedroom. Whoops! Did I really just say that? What must you think of me?'

Actually, Craig Norton thought quite a lot of the voluptuous Tara Jones. 'Tara, would it be alright if I were to take the chest away. I do think it could prove important to my investigations.'

'Well, yes of course. I hate it. What exactly is the purpose of your investigations?'

'To try and put an end to these strange events before anything really serious happens. Simon Clark-Mathos-predicted all this. He laid a curse fifty years ago, which has come home to roost. I guess he chose that length of time hoping that people's memories would fade and that he would be a very old man, or indeed dead, when it transpired. I hope I really can put an end to it.'

Of course, something really serious had already happened. Debbie Barry sat on the nursery floor, crying, waiting for the police to call.

From the back of a taxi, the wooden chest from the hotel in the boot, Craig Norton watched as two police cars sped in the opposite direction. He knew this was not a good sign.


# Chapter 14

'Mr Rawlson, I have some good news for you. The doctor said that, providing you have someone at home to look after you, the consultant is definitely going to allow us to discharge you today.' The staff nurse smiled.

Dennis Rawlson found it hard to raise a smile. His hospital bed had been a safe haven.

'Oh, come on, Mr Rawlson. That's really good news!'

Dennis forced a smile. 'I'll need to call my friend, Mr Lomes. He'll be coming to collect me. What sort of time do you think that will be?'

'Around five, I should think. I'll arrange for a telephone to be brought to your bedside.'

Rita Rawlson wandered the town, her mind fogged. Everywhere she went seemed to be a cruel reminder of what she had done. The display of kitchen knives in the window of the ironmonger's, the book on famous murder cases in the window of the book shop, the 'A' board outside the newsagent's announcing:

'BODY FOUND BY RIVER. SUSPECT HELD.'

Every time she closed her eyes, she could see that wretched symbol and underneath, those words: 'You failed. Try again.'

Knowing she wouldn't be welcome at the Ship and Anchor, Rita bought a half-bottle of vodka from the off-licence and made her way home, where an hour later, much of the contents of the bottle were gone. She fell to her knees on the kitchen floor, her hands covering her face, and sobbed, 'I can't do it, I just can't.'

In another hour, the rest of the bottle was gone and Rita's mood had changed from remorse to anger. She had received a call from Ken Lomes, informing her that Dennis was being discharged and was going to stay at the pub. Half an hour later, she was asleep, until something woke her, something in the room with her.

Craig Norton struggled through the back door of his aunt's flat with the chest from the hotel. Indeed, he had thought a good deal about the chest during the short taxi ride.

'Craig what on earth is that?'

'It's from the hotel, Mary. It belonged to the grandmother of the landlady. It's undoubtedly connected in some way with what has been going on in the town. It once belonged to Simon Clark-Mathos, the Master of the Brethren of the Visiting Spirits, is my guess.'

Mary lit a cigarette from a freshly opened packet, her fifteenth cigarette that day. 'I don't like it, Craig. There's something not nice about it.'

'Well, I'll keep it in my room for the time being. Tara, the landlady, has never opened it. She was afraid to.'

'Tara is very wise, I reckon. Gorgeous too, you know, and a great businesswoman. Worth a few quid, I should think. Make someone a lovely wife if they were willing to take on the hotel.' Mary didn't need to tell her nephew that Tara Jones was gorgeous.

The police had been at Debbie Barry's house for half an hour. Two uniformed male constables and a male and female detective. All the obvious questions had been asked, including, 'Did you leave the baby alone in the house at any point?' and, knowing that Debbie was a divorcee, 'Have you had any recent contact with the child's father?'

They felt it significant that she had fallen asleep. Maybe someone had got in as she dozed? How then would they get out with the baby, now disturbed and probably crying, the bright young female detective had pointed out. But what of the voices on the baby monitor? Local radio interference, the male detective had suggested. Then there was that symbol. If they had spoken to the local beat Constable Bardon, that would be less of a mystery. Of course, they were well aware of the peculiar events that had been occurring in the town and they assured Debbie that they would be speaking with PC Bardon. They also told Debbie that the details would be shared with other police forces around the country and that door-to-door inquiries would be carried out and a search team set up. All of this, little comfort for a distraught mother. In addition, they would arrange for a headline and appeal in the local paper whose evening edition would not yet have gone to press.

Rita Rawson awoke with a start. She was lying on her living room floor. Her head ached, her body ached. What time of day was it? In fact, what day was it?

'Rita Rawlson. Pleased to make your acquaintance at last!'

Rita rolled over and raised herself to a sitting position, her eyes gradually focusing. In front of her stood an old man, his heavily lined face framed by a carefully manicured grey beard, his hair, long and grey, pulled back across his head. He wore a black suit and a long black leather coat that reached almost to the ground.

Rita stumbled to her feet and collapsed back onto the sofa. 'Who are you? How did you get in?' It was then that she noticed the silver symbol that hung by a heavy chain around his neck, a symbol she at once recognised: an inverted five-pointed star surrounded by a circle, with a reversed 'Z' at its centre.

'I represent the Brethren of the Visiting Spirits. I assume you got my note yesterday?'

'Got it, ignored it, screwed it up and threw it away. The voice on the telephone ... that was you too, wasn't it? I don't know how you managed to get inside my head. I nearly killed my husband.'

'That's the problem. You *nearly* killed your husband. We want him dead.'

Rita began to feel sick. She needed a glass of water, but more than that she wanted this freak to leave. 'Why do I have to do your dirty work, you bloody weirdo?'

'Firstly, if you do it, there is no direct connection to my organisation. Secondly, you hate him.'

'And what exactly is your problem with my husband?'

'Ask him what his father did to us fifty years ago. We want revenge.' Rita leaned over the side of the sofa. She thought she was going to be sick. 'Very ladylike. Like you said, I got inside your head and I can do that anytime, Rita. I'll leave you now. By the way, you should always lock those balcony doors. You *will* do as I request.'

When Rita raised herself, the man was gone.


Mary Sharp lit another cigarette.

Craig didn't mention it, although at some point he felt he would have to. 'Mary, I haven't told you what happened to me inside the old Empire Ballroom earlier.'

Three cigarettes later, Mary had heard all about her nephew's strange experience that day.

'I have to do something, Mary. Thhis has to stop before something serious happens.'

Mary stubbed out her cigarette in the ashtray that was always full and a permanent feature in the middle of the kitchen table.

'I think it might already have happened, Craig. You haven't heard then? A baby has been taken from its cot in broad daylight.'

# Chapter 15

The evening edition of the local paper had been published. Outside, *Stonypool News*, the 'A' board displayed the latest headline:

'BABY TAKEN FROM COT. POLICE SEARCH LAUNCHED.'

In front of the board stood an old man with an immaculately trimmed beard and long grey hair, wearing a black suit and a long black leather coat. Around his neck, on a chain, hung the symbol of the Brethren of the Visiting Spirits. He began to laugh, a maniacal laugh that became louder and louder until the shopkeeper was drawn from behind his counter to see what was going on. The laughter stopped.

'Baby taken. I might have to buy a copy of that. The Brethren would love to see it!' he said out loud.

The shopkeeper rushed back inside the shop, picked up the telephone receiver and dialled. 'Hello. PC Bardon? It's George Simms over at *Stonypool News*. There's some weirdo outside laughing at the headline poster. Yes, the one about the missing baby. Yes, yes, I know that's not a crime, but he said something about "The Brethren" – whoever they are – would love to see it. No, doesn't seem right, does it? A description? Close-cropped beard, long grey hair, old long leather coat and some sort of medallion around his neck. A symbol, yes. An inverted five-pointed star surrounded by a circle, with a reversed 'Z' at its centre. No, he's gone now.'

Ken Lomes pushed the wheelchair, in which sat a very subdued Dennis Rawlson, through the front door of the Ship and Anchor. Julie, the barmaid, rushed from behind the bar to help.

'Dennis, your wife has called for you a couple of times.'

'Did she sound angry?'

'No. Not at all. Quite the opposite in fact.'

Ken pushed the wheelchair to the bar. 'You'd best call her, Dennis. Just to prepare the ground, you know.' He lifted the hatch in the bar, picked up the telephone, and placed it in front of his friend.

Reluctantly, Dennis lifted the receiver and dialled his home telephone number. Two minutes later, the call was over and Dennis looked confused.

Ken placed a double whisky in front of him. 'How did it go?'

'All right, I suppose. Full of apologies. Tried to blame the menopause, but even I know that happened for her years ago. She must think I'm stupid. What she is does start with an 'M' though: moody, mad cow. She asked me a really strange question about my father. Something about him having upset some people fifty years ago.'

Ken refilled his friend's glass.

'And do you know anything about it, Dennis?'

Dennis emptied his glass in one draw.

'Well yes, I do. I was a young lad at the time. My father, like me, was an important figure on the local council. There was a group of what he described as freaks who wanted to use the Empire Ballroom for one of their, as he described it, "Weird gatherings". He told me it was to do with the occult and they would be allowed over his dead body. It nearly came to that. He had death threats posted through the letterbox. In the end, he felt he had no choice but to allow it.

'The gathering went ahead – but weeks after they had scheduled it for. It ended in disaster. There was a fire at the ballroom. Lots of people died. They perversely blamed my father, claiming that if it had occurred on the original date they had planned, the fire would almost certainly not have happened. They also claimed it had ruined their reputation.'

'I've just thought of something! Remember when we were on the pier and that paddle steamer docked? Well, that guy waved a ticket at me and asked for directions to the Empire Ballroom. The symbol on that ticket … it was the same as on the head of the paper on which he received the death threats!' Dennis held up his glass for a refill. 'The Brethren of the Visiting Spirits. I remember now. Reckoned they could talk to the spirits, maybe even raise the dead.'

The door swung open. Ken looked up from the bar.

'Bloody hell, Dennis, look!'

In the doorway, dressed in nothing more than a white sheet stood Frank Chapley.

## Chapter 16

PC Bardon had managed a somewhat short discussion with Craig Norton at the police station, interrupted as it was by telephone calls about missing babies and strange men outside newsagents.

Craig had given the constable the book detailing the visit of the Brethren of the Visiting Spirits to Stonypool. He had also thanked him for his suggestion to visit Tara Jones, and explained that he had taken the wooden chest away. 'Lovely girl, PC Bardon. Thinks a great deal of you.'

'Yes indeed, Mr Norton, er, Craig. You will let me know of any developments, won't you? You are aware there's a baby missing and that there was that symbol scratched onto the paint on the headboard of the cot?'

Craig had turned to leave.

'Well yes, I was aware of the missing baby, but not the symbol on the cot. Thank you, PC Bardon. Thank you very much.'

An hour later, Bardon was sitting on a sofa at the Beach View Hotel, comfortably close to Tara Jones.

'That was a nice young man you sent to see me earlier. He took that horrible chest away. I'm not sure what he's going do with it. Like I told you earlier, I don't even know what's in it.' She slid even closer to the young constable. 'So, to what do I owe the honour of this visit? You don't normally call in to see me unless I ask.'

'Well, Tara, I could make up an excuse about requiring more information about my ongoing inquiries on things that have been happening to you and others, but no ...' PC Bardon blushed and swallowed, 'it's something you said earlier, Tara. Would you like to join me for a drink sometime?'

Before Tara could respond, the bell on the reception desk rang. 'Hold on there, my lovely. I'll be back very soon.'

At the reception desk stood a man with a heavily lined face, close-cropped beard, long grey hair and wearing a long black leather coat. Around his neck was a chain and from that chain hung a medallion bearing a symbol Tara recognised.

'Good afternoon, sir. Can I – '

'Young lady, you have something that belongs to me I think?'

Tara guessed to what he was referring. 'I did, but I don't have it anymore … if it's that horrendous wooden chest you're talking about? Anyway, how did you know I had it?'

His fixed stare was making Tara nervous. 'Oh, I know a great deal about you.' For a few moments he just stood and stared deep into Tara's eyes. She felt he had somehow touched her very soul. 'You have the Master's eyes, Tara.'

Tara had to make a physical effort to escape the strange man's gaze. 'I warn you, there's a policeman in the back room.'

Tara turned away from the reception desk and called out, 'PC Bardon, can you come out here please?' She turned to face the man who had so unsettled her, but he was gone.

Bardon stood next to her, prepared for conflict, but finding Tara alone said, 'Yes, Tara. How can I help? You look very pale.' He placed a hand on her arm. She was shaking. 'Tara, whatever is the matter?'

Tears welled in her eyes, and she threw her arms around the smitten young policeman. For several seconds she held him tight, only reluctantly releasing her grip on him. 'Sorry. I'm so sorry. I shouldn't have done that – only you make me feel safe.'

Bardon took her left hand in his right. 'Tara, don't apologise, honestly. You know I'll always help you if I can. Now come and sit down and tell me what's upset you.'

Tara smiled an uneasy smile. 'I'm going to lock the front door first.'

She explained her encounter with the old man, emphasising that the symbol he wore on a chain around his neck was the same as the one on her earrings and on the lid of that strange wooden chest.

'The Brethren of the Visiting Spirits?'

Tara frowned. 'Yes, that was the name of the society. How did you know that?'

'Craig Norton told me. He loaned me a book that contains information about them and their leader, Simon Clark-Mathos.'

At the mention of that name, Tara shuddered.

'PC Bardon, and I really can't keep on calling you that, there's something I want to tell you, but you're going to need a drink. I know I do. And yes, I would love to go for a drink with you, and this seems like the ideal opportunity. When are you off duty?'

The colour had come back to Tara's cheeks. Bardon looked at his watch.

'Officially, as of five minutes ago, and you can call me Steve. I need to go and change out of my uniform, but I'm worried about leaving you alone. Tara smiled sweetly.

'So what are you suggesting, Steve?'

'Well, my civvy clothes are at the police station. Come back with me in the car. I can get changed and then we can walk back and have a drink at the Ship and Anchor. To be honest, it's probably best for me to be in town this evening.'

Tara had already rounded up her coat and handbag.

'Well, there's no guests at the moment, so yes, that would be perfect!'

## Chapter 17

Debbie Barry had hardly moved from her armchair since the disappearance of her baby. She had been unable to eat and could barely speak. With her was a female police constable who was there more for emotional support than for any policing purposes. Only a few words had been exchanged between them, but Debbie was glad she was there. It had now been some hours and there had been no positive news. The WPC turned to look out of the front room window. Something had attracted her attention and she stood and pushed the net curtain that hung over the window to one side. Outside stood an old man with long grey hair and a neatly trimmed beard framing a heavily lined face. He wore a dark suit and a long leather coat. Around his neck on a chain hung a medallion, a symbol, an inverted five-pointed star surrounded by a circle, with a reversed 'Z' at its centre.

'Debbie, do you recognise that man outside?'

Debbie joined the WPC at the window.

The man stood only ten feet away. Debbie, legs weakening, collapsed onto the chair previously occupied by the female constable.

'Are you alright, Debbie?'

The colour had drained from the young mother's face. 'No, not really. I don't recognise that man, but isn't that medallion he's wearing the same symbol as the one scratched on my son's cot?'

'You're right, Debbie!'

In those few seconds, the man had gone.

Debbie wiped a tear from her cheek with the back of her right hand.

'There's something I haven't mentioned, I don't know why, perhaps because I've blanked it out. But yesterday, and I really don't know how, I found my son out of his pram and on the ground. He seemed absolutely fine, but when I was changing him later in the day, I found a red mark on him. It looked like a small sore patch, but when I looked closer, it was a symbol, the same one as on the cot.'

Mary Sharp took a cigarette from the second pack she'd opened that day, and lit it with a cheap red plastic lighter. Craig Norton shook his head.

'Mary, your smoking must be costing you a fortune. And with no fortunes being told, I'm surprised you can afford it.'

Mary smiled, took the cigarette from between her lips, and said, 'Craig darling, if I was going to run out of money, I'd have seen it in my future by now.' She inhaled deeply, and as if in defiance, blew a bellowing cloud of smoke in Craig's direction, making him cough.

'Thanks, Mary. If that's how it's going to be, I'm going to my room. I have stuff I need to do.'

'You're welcome. In there with that awful chest!'

'It's nothing compared to how awful *your* chest will be if you keep on smoking the amount you do!' Mary just smiled and drew again on her cigarette.

Craig sat on the bed in the room that he was temporarily occupying in Mary's flat, contemplating the wooden chest that sat by the wall in front of him. What, he wondered, was inside it? Was Tara Jones' fear of opening it irrational? Possibly she feared she may discover some long-hidden truth about her family, or maybe she was just plain superstitious. *Well*, he thought, *I have no family connection to it and I'm not superstitious*.

With those thoughts in mind, he slid from the bed and knelt in front of the chest. There was no lock, simply a brass hasp and a toggle that could be turned to release it. Slowly he rotated the toggle and swung the hasp upwards, where, stiff from years of not being used, it stayed. For a moment he paused before opening the lid, then in one smooth movement he raised it.

The temperature in the room dropped, so much so that he was able to see his breath. From across the hallway, he could hear his aunt coughing violently. Inside the chest, towards the top, was a purple cloth. Craig folded it back and lifted out the first of the items it covered: a silver candlestick in which was a three-inch stub of black wax candle. Next, he lifted out a silver dish about eight inches across, embossed on the bottom of which was the symbol of the Brethren of the Visiting Spirits. Once again, he lowered his right hand into the chest and withdrew an old glass jar with a screw lid that contained something resembling fine ground ash. Placing that carefully upon the floor, he yet again lowered his right hand into the emptying chest.

His hand contacted a large item wrapped in cloth. Easing it to the centre of the floor of the chest and now using both hands, he lifted it out, placed it on the floor, and started to carefully remove the dark purple cloth in which it was wrapped. Tilting the item backwards to free the cloth from underneath, he pulled it away. His heart leapt into his throat.

He was looking into the face of a skull, a human skull, mottled, discoloured, many years old he guessed. He paused before lifting the final item from the chest, a small book, seemingly bound in brown leather. On its cover, looking as if it had been branded into the binding material, was again the symbol of the Brethren of the Visiting Spirits. He placed it on the floor next to the other items which he surveyed as he raised himself up and sat upon the bed.

What Craig hadn't noticed is that he had been being watched by a girl, soaking wet, her thin white dress clinging to her body, her long dark hair clinging to her face.

## Chapter 18

PC Steve Bardon, arm in arm with Tara Jones, entered the saloon bar of the Ship and Anchor, to be greeted by a less than happy Ken Lomes.

'Good evening, constable ... Tara. So, what do you know about what's going on in this town. Weird stuff happening. Missing babies.' He gave a wry smile. 'And what about Dennis? His wife went completely mad. Not the first time though.' Ken's mood was lifting a little. 'Lovely to see you two together. Make a great couple you do.'

Sitting at a table by a window, Tara looked out at the promenade and the unsettled sea beyond. Without turning to look at Steve, in a hushed voice, she said, 'Steve, that thing I wanted to tell you ...'

Steve Bardon raised a hand and gently placing it on her chin turned her pretty face towards his.

'Yes, Tara?' Their eyes locked.

'It's like this, Steve. I think I might be responsible for what's going on in this town. All this weird stuff.' Steve put his pint back on the table and for a moment just looked at Tara in silence.

'Tell me, how could you possibly be responsible?' Tara wiped a tear from her cheek with the back of her left hand.

'You see, Steve, it's like this. I think I'm Simon Clark-Mathos' daughter, the leader of that society, the Brethren of the Visiting Spirits.'

In the public bar of the Ship and Anchor, Dennis Rawlson was becoming increasingly drunk. He blamed his lack of temperance on the unexpected sight of the late Frank Chapley, who, as suddenly as he had appeared, donning no more than a white sheet, had simply turned around, and as far as Dennis could tell just vanished.

Rita Rawlson stared at the reflection of her face in the bathroom mirror. It wasn't a pretty sight. That made her angry, and the more she looked, the angrier she became. *This is all Dennis' fault*, she thought, as she turned away from the mirror. 'Yes, Dennis,' she said out loud.

In the bedroom she and Dennis shared, she sat in front of the dressing table mirror, attempting to tidy her make-up. She stood, straightened her dress and went out to the hallway where she picked up the telephone receiver and dialled the number of the Ship and Anchor. 'Hello Ken. It's Rita Rawlson. Do you have a table available tonight? I'd like to have dinner with my husband.'

As the evening drew on and the temperature outside steadily dropped, there were few folk to notice the strange blue almost purple light forming once again over the old Empire Ballroom or hear the shouts and screams coming from within.

Moira Taggart had ventured down to the museum to assess the recent damage from what appeared to have been a break-in, but for which the police could find no sign of forced entry. The section of the museum dedicated to the history of fishing in the town seemed to have received the most attention from whoever or whatever the intruders were. This was of course the area where artefacts from the long-demolished fishermen's cottages were displayed, and among those artefacts had been the items used to ward off evil from the dwellings: witch bottles, a child's shoe, and others. Although the glass display cabinets remained locked, the glass intact, all these particular artefacts were gone, and Moira had a strong sense as to why. Turning her back on the display, she walked the few paces to the wall upon which the light switch was installed. Flicking the switch off, she became aware of the pungent smell of pipe smoke. She turned to look back the way she had just come. There was a shuffling sound in a far corner, and a man's gruff voice spoke.

'Thank you, sweet lady. We are forever grateful to you for saving our talismans, and when all this is over, we shall return them.'

Moira wasn't scared. She didn't even switch the light back on, just took a breath and said, 'You're very welcome. I trust you will be safe this night and hope this will soon all be over, and that the living of the town will be free of what I fear is a curse forever.'

She heard footsteps approaching on the wooden floor, the smell of pipe tobacco became stronger. Then she felt what could only be the kiss of a bearded man upon her cheek.

In the public bar of the Ship and Anchor, Ken Lomes had some bad news for his best friend, Dennis Rawlson. 'Erm, Dennis, there's something I need to tell you.'

'Yes, Ken? Another whisky please. And what is it?'

Ken faced away from Dennis towards the optics behind the bar and charged a glass with a double whisky. And without turning back to look at his wheelchair-bound friend, he said, 'Rita is going to be joining you for dinner tonight. She rang. I mean, what could I say?'

'No! Bloody no! That's what you could have said, Ken! Call her back and say I'm not feeling great and have gone to bed.'

Ken turned and looked nervously towards the door of the bar. 'I think it's too late for that, Dennis. She's here. Anyway, don't worry. If things turn nasty, PC Bardon is in the saloon bar.'

As indeed he was.

# Chapter 19

'Tara, I don't really know what to say. Are you being serious?' Steve Bardon lifted his pint from the table. The beer mat came with it.

'Steve, I certainly wouldn't say it for effect or as some kind of sick joke. No. Simon Clark-Mathos could be a very charming man apparently. He charmed my grandmother and so it seems my mother too. Growing up, I was aware that I looked very different to my sister. I just had a feeling. So many little signs. It would just make sense. And tonight when that strange man commented on my eyes.'

Steve put down his drink and placed a now cold hand upon Tara's. 'Sweetheart, even if you were, and you don't know that for sure, how could that make you responsible for anything that's happened?'

Another tear rolled down the hotel landlady's cheek. 'Because I'm his daughter. Because I am in possession of that chest. Because maybe they want me, this Brethren of the Visiting Spirits.'

Steve squeezed her hand. 'Tara, that organisation doesn't exist anymore, hasn't for years. According to Craig Norton's book, Mathos laid down the curse upon this town fifty years ago, well before you were even born.'

'Yes Steve, but who was that man who came to the hotel earlier, claiming to know things about me?' Tara drew a sharp breath, her pretty eyes widening. 'The man who's just come into the bar!'

Sauntering towards the bar was indeed Tara's visitor from earlier that day. For a moment he paused and stared directly into her eyes. At that exact same moment Rita Rawlson swung open the door to the saloon bar.

Craig Norton was packing the strange items back into the chest, all that is except the small book, which, once the other items were packed and the lid of the chest closed, he turned in his right hand, then back again. He was about to open the strangely bound cover when he heard a choking cough followed by another, then another, and then a breathless, short 'Craig!'

His aunt. Something was wrong with Mary!

Placing the book on top of the chest, Craig hurriedly swung open the bedroom door and ran to the kitchen where he found his aunt sitting at the table, her head in her hands, elbows on the table, red-faced, tears running down her cheeks, her breath being drawn in short rasping gulps. Craig stood behind her and rubbed her back with his right hand in a fruitless circular motion.

Mary spoke in a voice, thin and reedy. 'Craig, it was horrible. It was like I was being strangled by invisible hands.' She turned in her chair and put her right arm around Craig's waist. After a couple of minutes, her' breathing eased. 'I bet you thought it was the bloody cigarettes, didn't you?'

Craig smiled. 'Well, yes, it was only natural to assume.'

From the bedroom Craig had left a few moments earlier came the sound of fluttering and then a soft thump followed by the clunk of the lid of that recently closed wooden chest being raised to rest against the wall behind.

Steve Bardon turned his head in the direction of Tara Jones' gaze. He saw no man, only the red-faced and slightly swaggering Rita Rawlson, who realising the young constable was looking directly at her quickly turned and exited the bar by the door that she had only just come through.

Ken Lomes looked up from the glass he was drying with a cloth behind the bar. He forced a smile as he delivered his false, friendly greeting. 'Rita how lovely to see you!'

Rita Rawlson nodded. 'Good evening, Ken. And where will I find my beloved husband?'

Ken raised his arm and placed the glass on the shelf above the bar. 'He's out the back Rita. I'll let you through.'

Tara Jones was trembling. Had she imagined she'd seen that man again? That man she now felt sure was pursuing her. Pursuing her because she was the daughter of Simon Clark-Mathos, and because she was the person who now possessed that terrible chest of secrets that were now not so secret.

Steve Bardon raised himself from his chair, stood behind the seated Tara and put his arms around her. 'Tara darling, you're shaking. Are you alright?'

She certainly felt a great deal better enveloped in the arms of the handsome young policeman. 'I'm fine, Steve. Just my imagination, I guess. Can we go back to mine now? I'm really feeling quite tired.'

## Chapter 20

Outside the old Empire Ballroom, an elderly couple in a tatty Morris had pulled up at the opposite kerbside. The driver turned to look through his window. 'That's odd, Margaret. Look!'

His wife turned awkwardly in her thick faux fur coat.

'Look at what, Sid? It's an old ballroom, disused at that.'

Sid wound down the window and moved his face towards the gap.

'Look up, woman. Look up!'

Margaret raised her ample body over Sid's lap, making him groan.

'Bloody hell, woman! I can hardly breathe!'

For a moment, Margaret just stared upwards.

'Oh my goodness! What is that, Sid, and what on earth does that man think he's doing?'

On the roof of the ballroom stood a man, arms outstretched. A man in a long black coat over which hung a medallion on a chain. An inverted five-pointed star surrounded by a circle, at its centre a reversed 'Z'. The man was silhouetted in front of a blue almost purple glow that seemed to extend way into the sky.

Sid wound up his window and his wife moved her bulk back into the passenger seat. 'I don't know, Margaret. If the place wasn't so clearly disused, I would have thought it was some sort of promotion for a forthcoming show.'

Neither husband nor wife had noticed the empty wheelchair in a side street next to the ballroom. Sid started the engine of the ageing Morris. And leaving behind a cloud of blue smoke, husband and wife went on their way, discussion about what they had just seen turning to contemplation of supper and what delights they would watch on the television that evening, which led inevitably to the same old argument, always started by Margaret, about upgrading their old black and white set to one of the new colour ones like her sister had.

'Well, where is he then?' A disgruntled Rita Rawlson stood in a back room of the Ship and Anchor pub.

'I can assure you he was in here, Rita. He can't go far. He can barely move ten feet in that wheelchair.'

Ken Lomes opened the door onto the passageway that led to the private kitchen and toilet. He called out, 'Dennis. Dennis?' There was no reply. He switched on the passageway light.

The door at the end which led to the small rear courtyard was open, and as he moved towards it, he could see that the gate in the rear wall of the courtyard was open too. After securing both gate and door, Ken Lomes returned to a now furious Rita.

'He's gone, hasn't he, or should I say *wheeled himself away* to escape from me. I'll kill him!'

Well, she could have, if someone else hadn't already done the job for her.

In the midst of their black and white versus colour debate, the henpecked Sid had taken the wrong turning off the seafront road. And now the old Morris was heading back the way they had come, but one street up from the seafront, and they were just about to pass the rear of the old Empire Ballroom.

'I'm telling you, Sid, we could easily afford the rental on a colour set. That black and white one is making my eyes bad, I swear.'

Sid applied the brakes sharply, skidding to a halt and catapulting his complaining wife partially into the footwell, her sheer bulk preventing her from entering it entirely.

'Sidney, what did you do that for?'

'Well, clearly our telly hasn't affected *my* eyesight. Look in the road.'

Easing herself awkwardly back into her seat, Margaret scrunched her eyes and peered into the road directly in front of the car. 'It's a man, Sid, a man. You didn't hit him, did you?'

Sid turned off the engine. 'Of course I didn't. You would have known if I did. He was already there, lying in the road.'

Margaret shuddered. 'You don't think he's dead, do you?'

Sid snapped, 'How would I know, woman. Give me a chance to get out and look.'

The motionless body of a stout man, his right leg in plaster, blood pooling around his downward-facing head, was illuminated in the headlights of the old Morris. He was dead. Dennis Rawlson was dead.

Sid walked around to the passenger window of his car as Margaret wound it down. 'It doesn't look good. We passed a phone box a couple of hundred yards back. You stay here and I'll go and call 999. Oh, and you can take that coat off and put it over him.'

Margaret grunted. She shuffled out of the car, a selfish thought coming to her. If she had to buy a new coat, that would be nearly a year's rental on a colour television.

## Chapter 21

'What was that noise in your room, Craig?'

Mary Sharp had recovered from her strange strangulation ordeal, although her voice was still strained and croaky.

'I really don't know, Mary. Sit there and I'll take a look.'

In the small bedroom, the lid of the chest was open, as was the book which lay face down on the floor. In the middle of the bed, on top of the cloth it had been wrapped in, was the skull. On the floor between the bed and the chest was a pool of water. The room was freezing cold. Picking the book up from the floor, Craig turned it over. Still open at the page at which it had fallen, he sat on the bed and began to read aloud:

'Then we shall take the skull of a virgin and place it upon the altar and surround it with some ashes from the body from which it was taken. The candle should be lit, and the incantation chanted. They shall rise again among the living. Come back to us, come back to us, that we may take from you the strength we need this night to bring back your brothers and sisters to walk among us and spread our word.'

There was a scream, then a shout from the kitchen. Throwing down the book, Craig swung open the bedroom door and took the few steps to the kitchen at speed. Mary sat, her eyes wide, staring into a corner where a semi-opaque shadow-like form, the size of a man, was forming. As Craig watched, it developed a faceless head, arms and then feet, below what appeared to be the hem of a cloak, a cloak upon which hung a clearly defined silver chain to which was attached a medallion, the symbol of the Brethren of the Visiting Spirits. *Maybe I shouldn't have read that incantation aloud*, he thought.

Rita Rawlson jabbed the key into the lock of the front door of the house she had shared with her husband Dennis for fifteen turbulent years. She swung the door back with such force that the plant stand in the hallway rocked and deposited the potted plant which it supported onto the wooden floor with a crash of breaking china and a spray of earth. She muttered under her breath, 'Dennis, bloody Dennis!'

Kneeling down to pick up the pieces of the shattered pot, Rita noticed a piece of paper upon the floor that had been blown several feet along the hallway by her ungainly entry. Picking it up and turning it over, she immediately recognised the symbol printed at its head. With a lack of emotion, she read the words written below:

'You seem unable to carry out our will, so we took it upon ourselves to do what was required.'

As Rita stood up, there was a purposeful knock upon the front door. She had guessed who her unexpected visitors were.

'Good evening, madam, I'm Sergeant Innes and this is Constable Howard of North Haven Constabulary. It's about your husband. Can we come inside?'

Rita Rawlson did her best to look and sound shocked. Sergeant Innes delivered the news of her husband's death in the way that only an experienced policeman can, and as the pair left, with the observational skills that only policemen have, he saw the note from the Brethren of the Visiting Spirits on the small table by the telephone. He recognised the symbol printed upon it from the previous day's briefing. He picked up the note and put it in his pocket.

It wasn't an easy night for some of the residents of Stonypool. Ken Lomes had learned of the death of his best friend when the Morris-owning Sid and his wife, Margaret, had called into the Ship and Anchor for a drink to steady their nerves and told him of the body, its leg in plaster, that they had nearly hit in the road. Ken had soon put two and two together and made four

Craig Norton didn't sleep well after the appearance of the dark figure in the kitchen, which took some minutes to fade away. He sat up with his aunt until the early hours of the morning, as she couldn't sleep either.

Moira Taggart, strangely excited by her experience at the museum, found it impossible to settle and was out of her bed again in the early hours.

Steve Bardon and Tara Jones had managed some sleep together in Tara's bed.

# Chapter 22

## Day Four

Craig Norton left his aunt asleep at the kitchen table. By a little after half past nine, he was sitting at a table by the window of Seashells Cafe. Big Tony was delighted to see him and equally delighted that he had some news that Craig probably had not heard.

He withdrew a chair from below the table and sat down opposite. 'Yeah, last night an old couple found a body in the road. Turns out it was Rita the Cheater's husband, Dennis.'

Craig sipped the coffee that Big Tony had brought over for him. 'More, as you describe it, weird shit. Tony, it's getting worse, and through what I've learned, I reckon we have another two days and nights of it to contend with. And who knows what that might mean. Another death? Maybe more than one.'

Big Tony smiled. 'Two more days of weird shit. Could be good for business. Already more folk in town than usual for the time of year. Ghoulish lot the English.'

Craig shook his head. 'No, Tony. It has to stop, and I think I know a way it could be done, but I will need your help.'

Steve Bardon pulled on his trousers, leant over and kissed a slumbering Tara on the forehead. She opened her eyes and smiled. 'Good morning, lovely. I'm afraid I'm due on duty in half an hour. I'll call in during my shift to make sure you're alright.'

Tara moaned softly. 'You sure you can't stay? No, of course, I'm being silly. I'll miss you!'

Twenty minutes later, Bardon arrived at Stonypool Police Station. Once inside, he played back the first message on the answering machine:

'Message for PC Bardon. This is Sergeant Innes from North Haven Police. We were called to your patch last night to deal with a body, a Dennis Rawlson. Could you give me a call on 425 437. I need to talk to you about his wife. It's now half past six.'

Steve Bardon changed into his uniform trousers and shirt, filled the kettle, and smiled at the thought of his night with the lovely Tara. Poor Dennis' death weighed on his mind though. He picked up the telephone receiver and dialled the number that Sergeant Innes had left him on the station answering machine.

'Hello. Sergeant Innes.'

'Good morning, sir. It's PC Bardon at Stonypool here.'

'Ah, yes. Dennis Rawlson lived and worked on your patch. Found dead in the road last night by an elderly couple from out of town. Massive head trauma, so it doesn't look accidental. Found something at his wife's house that I think I'd like you to see.'

'Okay, sir. I can come to you, or you could come to me.'

'Thanks, Bardon. I'll come down to you. I need to show you where the body was found. It's been a very long night. You can buy me breakfast too. Be with you in half an hour.'

'Very good. See you soon, sir.'

An hour later PC Bardon and Sergeant Innes were sitting at a table in Seashells Cafe, cooked breakfasts and steaming cups of tea in front of them. Sergeant Innes pulled a small piece of note-paper from the inside pocket of his tweed jacket.

'Look at this, Bardon. I picked it up at the Rawlson place last night when we went round to deliver the bad news to his wife. You recognise the symbol on it of course. We do from your very comprehensive notes relating to stuff that's been happening in this town.'

Steve Bardon took the note and read it. 'Yes. The Brethren of the Visiting Spirits. Not been active for forty-five years at least. If I were to take this note literally, I would deduce that Dennis had been killed and that Rita Rawlson knew about it.'

Through a mouthful of sausage, Sergeant Innes replied, 'Yes, Bardon.' He swallowed, picked up his cup and washed down the half-chewed food. 'I'm pleased you see it that way too.'

Big Tony sauntered up to the table with two plates of toast. He paused by the table. 'Crazy shit. Yeah, crazy.'

Sergeant Innes turned and glared at the cafe owner. 'I beg your pardon?'

Big Tony put the plates of toast down on the table. 'All this weird stuff that's happening. That's their symbol, isn't it, on that piece of paper. Those Visiting Spirits people?'

Sergeant Innes looked at Bardon and then back to Big Tony. 'And what do you know about these people, sir?'

'Only what that Craig Norton guy told me. He was in here this morning. Reckons he's got a plan to end all this madness. Not sure I want it to end just yet, been great for trade!'

Sergeant Innes turned to face Bardon. 'Who exactly *is* this Craig Norton, and what do you know about him? I saw him mentioned in your notes.'

Behind PC Bardon, at the next table, sat a man wearing a long leather coat and sporting long grey hair and a neatly trimmed beard. On a chain around his neck hung a medallion, an inverted five-pointed star surrounded by a circle, with a reversed 'Z' at its centre.

Craig Norton was indeed formulating a plan. 'Mary, this can't continue.'

'What's that, Craig?'

'All these things that are happening in Stonypool. I reckon that Dennis Rawlson's death was just another event caused by it.' Mary lit a cigarette and inhaled deeply, then blew out a cloud of smoke that engulfed her nephew's head. Craig coughed. 'Mary, I really am going to see to it that you give up smoking by the time I leave.' His aunt blew out another cloud of smoke in Craig's direction.

'Surely I'm allowed a little pleasure in life. Forty years I've been smoking and I'm not giving it up now.' Craig shuffled his chair round to escape the smoke.

'I have a plan, Mary, to end all this madness. I'm going to need your help though.'

# Chapter 23

Sergeant Innes and PC Bardon stood on the pavement next to the section of road where Dennis Rawlson's body had been found the night before.

'Just here it was, Bardon. Some of my colleagues in the CID reckon there was no crime committed. Think he was trying to walk unaided on that cast and fell heavily into the road. I'm not so sure. The head trauma was extensive. The old couple that found him reckon there was something odd happening on the roof of the old ballroom behind us. Said there were strange lights and a man standing up there about five minutes before they came across the body.

'If you ask me, we should take a look inside the place. I can't figure out why he would have got out of his wheelchair without crutches and struggled for several yards? Who could give us access to the ballroom?'

Bardon took a few moments to think. 'Well sir, after poor old Frank Chapley was found in there, the rear entrance was boarded over, but not very well. I'm betting we could try that way. Better let headquarters know what we're doing though.'

'Rubbish, Bardon. We're policemen carrying out investigations in the line of duty. That Chapley fellow? He's the old tramp they found dead in there, isn't he?'

'Yes sir.'

'This place is going to get a reputation!'

Tara Jones was late opening the front door of the hotel. She had needed to telephone her best friend, Marie, to tell her that she had finally hooked the handsome young policeman she had lusted after for nearly three months. With a smile on her face, she turned the key in the lock of the front door, which was immediately pushed open, propelling Tara backwards.

'Well, Miss Jones, we meet again!'

In front of her stood her visitor of the previous day, his medallion the first thing to register with Tara.

'What do you want?'

'To talk to you. No policeman here today. He's down at the cafe with one of his colleagues. Bungling idiots can't even recognise a crime scene when they see one. Can I come in?'

Before Tara had a chance to speak, her unwelcome visitor had walked past her and was standing by the reception desk. 'Miss Jones, Tara, you have something that belongs to me.' Tara was shaking.

'I told you before, I don't have it. You don't scare me!'

'I believe you, Tara, and anyway I think I know where it is and the person who has it is in big trouble. My intention is not to scare you. I mean you no harm. Quite the reverse. You are the last living blood relative of Master Simon Clark-Mathos. I've kept tabs on your whereabouts for twenty nine years. We need you. We want you to bear a child who in maybe twenty years' time will lead a new generation of the Brethren of the Visiting Spirits.'

Tara slumped into a chair by the reception desk.

'Twenty nine years? I'm nearly thirty years old. You mean to tell me you've been keeping tabs on me for most of my life? You must have time to waste Mr ...?'

'Nathaniel Masterton. Oh, not a waste. Besides I have plenty of time. I'm now over one hundred and twenty years old and may have many more ahead. I have a great deal to thank your father for.'

The reception area rang with the sound of maniacal laughter.

# Chapter 24

'Mary, that chest.'

'I told you, Craig, I'm not giving up smoking!'

Craig smiled broadly. 'Not *your* chest, Mary, the one I brought back from the hotel. Its contents are essential to my plan, but we can't keep it in your flat anymore. It's at the root of what has been happening to us. I need to find somewhere to store it for a couple of days.'

Mary removed the cellophane from yet another packet of cigarettes. 'What about my fortune-telling booth by the entrance to the pier? It's secure and reasonably dry.'

Craig's smile grew broader – if that were possible. 'Aunt Mary, you're a genius. If you have the keys, I'll take it down there now. By the way, feel free to have a cigarette to celebrate your clever thinking.'

Twenty minutes later, Craig was walking away from the little fortune-telling booth that now contained the chest and its contents. As he walked back along the promenade, he paused to look over the seawall. Unseen by him, a man with long grey hair, a neatly trimmed beard and wearing a long black leather coat and a medallion on a silver chain had sidled up next to him.

'Craig Norton, if I'm not wrong?'

Craig, startled, turned to face the man who stood next to him. 'Craig who? Never heard of him.' Craig recognised the medallion worn by the man immediately. He knew what he wanted.

'Don't mess me about, Mr Norton. I know who you are, and you have something that belongs with me. Something you took from Tara Jones. Am I right?'

Craig laughed 'Alright. So I am Craig Norton. And if you mean that weird chest, it's out there.' He raised his right arm, and with his index finger pointed out to sea.

Nathaniel Masterton placed a hand on Craig's shoulder.

'You had better be joking, young man, and I really hope for your sake you are.'

Craig brushed Masterton's hand away.

'What if I do have it? It belongs to Tara, but she doesn't want it near her.'

Masterton lowered himself and sat on the seawall. 'Allow me to introduce myself. I am Nathaniel Masterton, a faithful of the Brethren of the Visiting Spirits. I know you have heard of us.'

Craig sat down upon the seawall beside Masterton.

'Oh, indeed I *have* heard of the Brethren of the Visiting Spirits, *and* of you. That's if you are *actually* Masterton. He was born in 1850; that's one hundred and twenty years ago. If you are, you're looking good on it.' Craig could see the anger rising in Masterton's face.

'I am Masterton. The Master, Simon Clark-Mathos, granted me life sufficient to see the Brethren of the Visiting Spirits reformed, and to witness the results of his curse on Stonypool.'

'So, you come back here fifty years after Clark-Mathos placed his curse, which is now coming true. It makes sense, I suppose. So, tell me something about that organisation that I don't know.'

Masterton dug his fingernails into the concrete wall which had been softened by years of coastal weather. 'Tara Jones is the daughter of Simon Clark-Mathos, his last surviving blood relative in fact.' Unwittingly, Nathaniel Masterton had just given Craig Norton the final element of his plan to rid Stonypool of the regime of evil that had descended upon it.


## Chapter 25

Sergeant Innes and PC Bardon stood behind the old Empire Ballroom. The boarding that covered the rear doors from which Craig Norton had run had at some point since been put back in place, but not nailed to secure it. Between them the two policemen lifted the heavy plywood sheet out of the way, placing it against the wall to the left beside one half of the double doors through which deliveries would have been taken in years gone by. It was unlocked. Bardon opened it a few inches and stopped, taking a step backwards.

Sergeant Innes grunted, 'What's the bloody matter, Bardon? Just open the bloody door for goodness' sake!'

Bardon moved towards the door and placed his ear against the gap. 'Sir, come here and listen. Bardon shifted sideways to allow the sergeant to stand close to the door.

From deep within the ballroom came the sound of a girl crying pitifully, while barely audible in the background came what sounded like chanting.

Sergeant Innes stood back. 'Sod this, Bardon!' Innes raised his right leg and kicked the door violently open, stepped inside and listened. Silence. 'Come on, Bardon. I don't know what's going on in here, but I'm bloody well going to find out.'

Bardon stepped inside. 'I wouldn't even want to guess, sir. All I know is that the things that have been happening in this town recently have opened my mind to alternative possibilities.'

'The supernatural Bardon. Is that what you're referring to? Get a grip of yourself, man. This is some weirdo with a tape player having a joke at other people's expense – though *why* is beyond me. Drugs maybe?'

Steve Bardon just knew those sounds had been no tape recording, and now he was intrigued. His eyes had adjusted to the dark. He slowly paced forward, debris crunching beneath his feet. 'Come on, sir. Let's take a look.'

Sergeant Innes caught up with the young constable. They walked along the dark passageway that led to the ballroom itself, Bardon keeping one hand against the left-hand wall to guide himself. As the pair got closer to the end of the passageway, the light seemed to improve, although its quality was somewhat strange. Moments later, the two officers stood in the opening at the end of the passageway, mouths open but in silence. The entire ballroom was illuminated by a blue almost purple glow.

Sergeant Innes was the first to break the silence. 'So, Bardon, somebody is in here. Why else would the place be lit up like this?'

Before Bardon could answer, The pair became aware of a dull thumping sound like a heartbeat. Second by second it became louder until it could be felt below their feet. 'Sir, look!' Bardon pointed up to the balcony of the ballroom where a woman stood, a woman whose features were barely discernible in the strange dull light.

The thumping sound grew louder and then stopped. The strange light grew stronger.

Innes called out, 'Hey you, madam, come down here. We're police officers and we need to speak to you.'

There was a piercing scream and the woman threw herself from the balcony, but somehow never reached the ballroom floor, vanishing in a bright flash of blue light.

'Bloody hell, Bardon! What just happened?'

'Well sir, like I said, some really strange things have been going on around here lately. It was you who used the word *supernatural*, not me, sir.'

Innes scowled. 'Don't be flippant, Bardon. That was an illusion, a stage trick. I don't deny that this place is weird though.'

Suddenly, the pair were plunged into darkness, but only for a couple of seconds. Electric lighting on the balcony turned on with a click of a switch. From which direction the sound came it was impossible to tell. In front of them stood a middle-aged man in a brown warehouse coat.

'Gentlemen, officers, welcome. I saw you arrive. Somewhat unorthodox method of entry though. I'm Vic Gaskill, sort of the custodian of this place. What can I do for you?'

Sergeant Innes snapped, 'Saw us arriving? So, you're responsible for that ridiculous charade we just observed!'

Vic Gaskill smiled. 'Ridiculous charade? I don't know what you mean Mr –?'

'I'm Sergeant Innes. And this, I'm sure you already know, is PC Bardon, your local beat constable. We're investigating the death of a local man, Dennis Rawlson. He was found in the road behind here last night. Are you able to offer us any information, Mr Gaskill?'

Gaskill shook his head. 'I'm afraid not, sergeant. I didn't even know there had been a death so close by.'

Sergeant Innes was becoming impatient. 'Didn't know, Mr Gaskill? You didn't see the police officers out there last night? Didn't notice the road closure today? Didn't hear of something on your own doorstep of such magnitude?'

'I'm sorry, Sergeant, PC Bardon. No, I didn't. Feel free to look around though. Shout out when you've finished.'

With that, Vic Gaskill turned to walk away, much to the annoyance of Sergeant Innes.

'Gaskill! Don't walk away; I need to talk to you.' Innes stepped forward and with his right hand reached out to grab Vic Gaskill by the shoulder. His hand passed right through, and the shocked policeman stumbled.

Gaskill laughed and then was gone.

## Chapter 26

Craig Norton smiled at Nathaniel Masterton. He knew that the steely resolve that Masterton relied upon to intimidate was weakening. 'And I suppose you know something about that missing baby, Mr Masterton?'

Masterton was angry. He needed to deal with this young upstart who was trying his patience. Of course he knew about Debbie Barry's missing baby.

'Fuck you, Norton. If you're that interested, I'll give you a clue. Page fifty-seven.' It took just a moment for Craig to realise to what Masterton was referring. 'I'll bid you good day, Mr fucking clever clogs Norton.'

With that, Masterton stood, turned, and began to walk away to the east along the seafront.

Craig turned to walk in the opposite direction, pausing momentarily to look behind him. Masterton had vanished. Five minutes later, Craig was unlocking the door of the little booth by the pier entrance that was now the temporary home of the chest. Looking behind himself, he stepped inside and pulled the door almost shut, leaving a gap to let in what little light the outside world could provide. Hastily, he opened the lid of the chest and took out the small leather-bound book and placed it inside his jacket. Ten minutes later he was back at his aunt's flat, thumbing through that same book until he had found page fifty-seven.

Ken Lomes dropped a pint glass on the bar floor. 'Shit! Sorry, Julie. I just can't believe he's gone. I'm telling you there's something odd about it. Why would he get out of his wheelchair and go wandering? Bloody Rita, I reckon, in which case I feel partly to blame as it was me who allowed her to come here last night.'

Julie grabbed the dustpan and brush from behind the bar, got down on one knee and began sweeping up the broken glass.

'Ken, that's just stupid. If she wanted to come here, she would have done so without your input.' She stood and tipped the remnants of the shattered glass into the bin.

'I don't know what to think, Julie. My head's all over the place. Hold on, who's that outside?'

The pair stared at a face leering through one of the front windows of the pub. It was the face of Nathaniel Masterton.

Debbie Barry sat alone, despite the concerns of the young WPC who had spent so much time with her since the disappearance of her baby. Debbie had assured her she would be fine. She wasn't feeling fine though, far from it. She had hardly slept, and in the short snatches of sleep she did have she dreamed that her son was back home, safe in his cot. But when she pulled the covers back, she saw that his face was that of the man she and the WPC had seen outside her house. There had been no updates from the police, and with every hour that passed Debbie's hopes weakened.

'Mary! You have to stop smoking, honestly.' Craig Norton was engulfed in a cloud of stinking blue smoke. 'And have you changed the brand you're smoking? They smell truly revolting.'

His aunt laughed. 'Yes, young man. A little harsher on the throat, but tuppence a packet cheaper.'

Craig raised himself from the kitchen chair in which he was sitting and made his way to his bedroom, book in hand. Sitting on the bed, his right-hand index finger in place at page fifty-seven, the young publisher's assistant opened the book and began to read:

*If the ceremony is intended to invoke the presence of a spirit of high order and be it that the intention is to restore life to that former earthly occupant, the invocation described previously in this volume will be followed but will include the sacrifice of a child below one year old. Upon such sacrifice and with ten drops of the child's blood being placed in the ceremonial bowl, the chanting of the name of the spirit to be returned shall be started, accompanied by the regular repetition of the words: 'Oh brother of the dark come back. Through us you shall live again.'*

Craig closed the book and sat in thought. So this is what Masterton was planning. This was the purpose of the abduction of the baby. He wanted to bring Simon Clark-Mathos back from the dead or, Craig thought, from some dark slumber from which he would be regaining his energy. Craig knew he had to be first, to beat Masterton at his own game to raise Clark-Mathos, but he couldn't harm a child. Indeed, he had dreamed of having children of his own. He couldn't help but think of the lovely Tara Jones. Yes, Tara, daughter of Clark-Mathos. Surely a good reason for Masterton to return? A blood relative, a close link to his Master, but now someone who had betrayed him by giving the things required for the service to another, to him, Craig Norton. Yes, he had most of what was required to raise the spirit of Clark-Mathos, all except a baby and the ability to kill. He had Tara on his side though surely? Could he persuade her to help? Maybe she was in danger? No, she was definitely in danger!

Constable Bardon and Sergeant Innes stood staring at the point where a moment ago the seemingly solid form of Vic Gaskill had stood.

'Bloody stage trickery, Bardon. Mind you, bloody good stage trickery. I suppose you'll be putting it down to the supernatural though?'

Bardon wasn't listening to his superior. His attention had been grabbed by an object that lay a few feet to the left of where Vic Gaskill had stood only moments before. 'Sir, look.' Bardon pointed to a metal pole around four feet in length. At one end was a circle formed of a gold-coloured material, within it an inverted five-pointed star, with a reversed 'Z' at its centre, both formed of the same material, but half was discoloured, tainted by what the young policeman guessed was dried blood.

'Who is that bloke, Julie?' Ken Lomes stared intently at the face of Masterton, framed by a small glass pane in of one of the pubs front windows.

Julie shuddered. 'I don't know, Ken, but he gives me the creeps.'

A moment later, Masterton was gone.

'I've seen him a couple of times, Julie. He's only been around here since all this weird stuff started happening.'

Julie smiled, relieved at Masterton's departure. 'Probably just some ghoulish weirdo attracted by the publicity the town has had since it all kicked off.'

Ken shrugged. 'Probably.' Although deep down he knew there was something evil about this man.

Debbie Barry looked at her face in the mirror which hung in the hallway of her house. A combination of despair, exhaustion and how terrible she looked caused her eyes to fill with tears. Turning away towards the front door she could see through the frosted glass at the top movement, as if somebody was standing on the step about to ring the bell. She waited. The bell didn't ring, but whoever it was, was still outside. Wiping the tears from her face with the back of a hand, she drew a deep breath and took the few paces to the front door, turned the latch, and slowly opened it.

A wizened, dishevelled old man wrapped in a grimy white sheet, his face a ghostly grey pallor, his feet bare, stood upon the step. Frank Chapley. Debbie was about to slam the door on this ghastly individual, but he said something that immediately stopped her.

'Your baby isn't dead.'

For a moment Debbie just stared at this strange old man before she was able to speak. 'My baby? What do you know about my baby? Who are you?'

'I just know he's not dead, that's all. My name is Frank Chapley.'

'If you know anything, you need to tell the police.'

'No, madam. I know for sure they would take no notice of me, Frank Chapley.'

Debbie thought she knew the name, had seen or heard it somewhere recently, but where? She shuddered. A chill ran through her body. She had seen his name in the local newspaper. Frank Chapley, the vagrant found dead in the old Empire Ballroom.

At that moment, her mind found it impossible to string together a rational sentence. Opening her mouth to speak, what arrived was a scream, followed by the words, 'Go away! You're dead!'

She slammed the door, and shaking ran to the telephone and picked up the receiver, immediately replacing it back in its rest. How could she possibly explain to the police that she had been visited by a dead man who had news regarding her missing child? She began to cry again.


## Chapter 27

Craig Norton placed the book on top of the chest that stood against the wall of his bedroom in his aunt's flat. He raised himself from the bed, opened the door and returned to the kitchen where Mary Sharp sat, cigarette in hand.

'Coffee, Aunt Mary?' Craig inquired.

'Oh, yes please, if you're making one for yourself.'

Three minutes later, aunt and nephew were sitting at the small kitchen table, steaming mugs in front of them. Mary took another cigarette from a half-empty pack and lit it. Craig scowled. Mary smiled. Craig took a sip of his coffee.

'Mary, I found out something about Tara Jones and I'm actually quite concerned for her safety.'

Mary drew hard on her cigarette and blew out a long plume of blue smoke, thankfully not in Craig's direction. 'Oh, have you? That girl's always been a bit of a mystery. Gorgeous though, isn't she? What is it you're worried about?'

Craig took another sip of his coffee. 'She's more connected to this whole strange business than I thought. Connected through bloodline in fact, and yes, she is gorgeous.'

His aunt stubbed out her cigarette in the already overfull ashtray. 'If you're that worried, why don't you go and see her? I reckon she gets lonely at that hotel – especially out of season.'

Craig drained his mug in one large gulp. 'Mary, I'm going to do exactly that!'

Fifteen minutes later he was standing outside the entrance to the Ocean View Hotel. He tried the door. It was locked. He reached up and jabbed at the bell push and could hear the faint sound of the bell inside. He waited. Nobody came to the door. Again, he jabbed at the bell push. This time, he sensed movement behind the door, which then opened a few inches to reveal Tara's face.

A man's voice, a voice that he recognised, called out from within the reception area, 'Whoever it is, tell them to go away!' It was Masterton.

Tara didn't speak. She swung the door open wide and beckoned him in. She led him to the hotel reception. There, slumped in a chair sat Masterton, looking fully ten years older than when he had last seen him only a few hours ago. Masterton glared at him.

'Craig fucking Norton. I might have guessed! Come here to schmooze the Master's daughter, have you? Or have you come to give me back my things?'

Craig gave an exaggerated laugh. 'There's no chance of that, Masterton. I read page fifty-seven and I know what you intend to use that baby for.'

Masterton gave a rasping cough, the cough of a man most unwell.

'Too bloody right, Norton. I'm dying. If I don't raise the Master, I shall be dead within weeks I reckon. Only he can grant me an extension to my life.'

With Masterton's attention diverted, Tara had gone into the small office behind the reception desk, picked up the telephone receiver and dialled the police station. Craig watched as Masterton attempted to stand, his strength clearly waning. Masterton's intentions were laid bare, Craig's ideas about why he so desperately wanted the chest returned now confirmed.

Tara reappeared from the back room. 'I've called the police station. They were very interested in your knowledge of the missing baby. Someone is on their way.'

Masterton, with one last effort, eased himself up to his full height. 'You fool! Do you really think the police worry *me, Nathaniel Masterton*? I have powers beyond any you can imagine. You mark my words; they will not make it here.'

## Chapter 28

At the old Empire Ballroom, Constable Bardon and Sergeant Innes stood over the bloodstained symbol.

'Bardon, that's definitely blood. I need to get a couple of my men down here straight away. There's a telephone box just up the road. I saw it on our way here. Just wait with that thing until I return.'

Bardon was looking back towards the passageway through which they had entered earlier, his eyes now accustomed to the strange light which almost unnoticed had filled the entire ballroom. 'Sir, look.' He pointed to some smeared marks along a line on the floor that was clear of dust. 'I didn't notice that earlier, sir. Looks like blood. I'd say Rawlson was killed in here and his body dragged and dumped outside.'

Sergeant Innes sneered. 'Fancy yourself as a detective, do you, Bardon? Leave the clever stuff to the boys in CID.' Innes walked away carefully so as not to disturb this new evidence.

Ian Murray, a young constable who had only recently completed his training and had been posted to Stonypool as a gentle introduction to policing, had taken Tara's call.

He threw on his uniform jacket and quietly made his way outside to the little Morris 1100 Panda car. It had been allocated to the station that morning and was less than two weeks old. When he had picked it up from the force vehicle workshop earlier that day, the workshop manager had joked that he didn't want to see it back there with dents to fix. Murray had laughed as he got in and adjusted the seat to accommodate his six-foot three-inch frame. He'd never driven a new car before, and he had smiled broadly as he had pulled out of the workshop gates. Now, driving carefully away from the police station, he had nearly reached the seafront.

It was stuffy in the little car and he wound down the window as he approached the junction which would take him onto the promenade. As he slowed to stop and the road noise diminished, he heard a sound that he really was not expecting: the chimes of an ice cream van. Stopping completely, the sound became increasingly louder. He looked carefully to his left and then to his right. Satisfied that no other vehicles were approaching, he pulled out. From the corner of his right eye, he saw a shape. He turned his head. There, bearing down upon his little nearly new vehicle was the colourful front of an ice cream van. The only possible way he could avoid a collision was to accelerate hard straight forwards so that it would pass behind him, assuming that the driver did not swerve to avoid him. He stood hard on the accelerator and the new and lively engine of the Morris picked up rapidly, somewhat more rapidly than Murray was expecting.

In a split second, he was hurtling across the road, mounting the pavement, and striking the seawall hard. Dazed, the young constable pushed open the driver's door, which creaked as the front edge of it scraped against the offside wing, which had been pushed backwards by the force of the impact. He raised himself shakily to his feet. He could still hear the chimes of an ice cream van, although no longer the music box-style chimes of 'Greensleeves', but another tune he recognised: Wagner's 'The Flight of the Valkyries'.

Masterton's coughing and wheezing stopped as he heard an ice cream van's unusual chimes pass by. He smiled broadly. 'So where's your policeman, Tara? Don't have to come far, do they!' He laughed mockingly, which brought on another fit of coughing. He sat down heavily.

'And where's a doctor for you, Masterton? The hospital's not far away, is it?' Craig Norton quipped and smiled at his comment.

Tara hid her smile with a pretty hand. For a moment, Masterton's coughing subsided.

'Fuck you, Norton. I want my stuff back and it's obvious you have it!' Taking a deep breath and rising to his full height, some of his usual strength regained, he rushed at Norton, pinning him against the wall by his throat. His breath, strangely icy cold blew upon Norton's face as he hissed some words: 'I'd worry about your aunt, Madame bloody Volatska if I was you. I know you're keeping my stuff at her flat and I can be there a lot quicker than you can!' With that Masterton walked out at a frantic pace.

'I'll run you to your aunt's place in the car.' Tara Jones was already scrabbling in her handbag for the keys.

Moira Taggart unlocked the front door of the museum. There was a strange, heavy atmosphere inside. She clicked the front door shut behind her and made her way to the dark, windowless museum through the raffia that hung down across the inner door. The atmosphere seemed even heavier there – but then it was always stuffier than the shop and pay desk area. Switching on the lights, she turned to her left towards the small library area that contained books of local interest. It was one of these she had come for. Behind her there was what sounded like a scraping of feet and a sigh.

Without turning, in a low voice, Moira said, 'Hello?'

For a moment there was silence and then, 'Hello to you, my darling.'

She knew the voice, she had heard it here before, recently. A firm hand was placed upon her right shoulder, the smell of tobacco smoke filled her nostrils. Moira turned to face the fisherman she had known to be there previously, although this time she could see him clearly. She felt calm and loved.

The fisherman took his pipe from his mouth, bent down, and kissed her gently on her left cheek. In his right hand he held a canvas bag, tied at the top. He placed it gently on the floor beside Moira. 'I'll leave this with you. Keep it here. When the time comes, you'll know who to give it to.'

Once again, he kissed Moira gently on the left cheek, then said, 'Goodnight, lovely lady, and thank you. We may meet again if this torturous period can be made to end, and I know you will take your part in that with pride.'

He placed his pipe back in his mouth and as Moira watched, he slowly faded away.

## Chapter 29

Mary Sharp sprayed air freshener and made her way out of the toilet to return to her favourite daytime haunt, the kitchen. On the way she lit yet another cigarette. Settling herself at the kitchen table, she pulled the overfull ashtray towards her and opened a copy of *Woman's Weekly*. Inhaling heavily on her cigarette, she then blew out a cloud of blue smoke. From behind her came a gravelly cough. She froze, the partially turned page of her magazine remaining that way.

'You know what, those bloody things will kill you. Mind you, if you don't tell me what I need to know, I'll save them the bother!'

Mary stood and turned, to be confronted by Nathaniel Masterton. She just stared.

'Lost for words are you, woman? Answer me this, where is the chest your nephew brought back here?' For a few seconds Mary remained silent. 'Well, Madame bloody Volatska, tell me, or the only fortune you'll be seeing is your own: six feet under in a wooden box!'

Mary's power of speech returned. 'I've no idea what you're talking about. And anyway, how did you get in here?'

'You should lock your doors. Anyway, never mind that, you stupid woman. Your nephew, Craig Norton, has that chest. And it belongs to me. Now tell me where it is before I take this flat apart!'

To Mary's relief she heard the sound of a key in the front door lock. A second later Craig Norton burst into the kitchen.

'Masterton! Leave her alone; she's nothing to do with all this. And anyway, what you want isn't here and I'm not about to tell you where it is.'

'I think otherwise, Norton. Now tell me where it is or you'll be attending a funeral!' Masterton coughed, then coughed again and again until his eyes were streaming, and, no longer able to stand, he collapsed into the chair that Mary had vacated. She was now sporting a fresh cigarette, the smoke from which she was deliberately blowing in Masterton's direction.

Craig smiled at his aunt. 'For once, smoking might be saving your life, Mary!'

'Who is this man, Craig?'

Masterson continued to cough uncontrollably.

'His name is Nathaniel Masterton, devotee of the Brethren of the Visiting Spirits. He has powers bestowed on him by his Master, but his time is running short and I'm going to see to it that it runs out sooner rather than later.'

Masterton had stopped coughing but struggled for breath. 'Fuck you, Norton!'

Five plain clothes officers with powerful torches stood on the dance floor of the old Empire Ballroom. They had contacted the elderly couple who had found Dennis Rawlson's body, who had now joined them at the venue, delighted to be involved in such a thing.

'I tell you, Sid, it's just like an episode of *Softly, Softly*, except that it's in colour. Are you listening, Sidney?' The henpecked Sid didn't answer, just shook his head. 'Didn't you see, Sidney? On the way down here, that television rental place is doing a special offer if you sign up this month?'

One of the officers approached them, and before he could speak, Margaret seized the moment. 'Do you have a colour television, officer? Everything is so much better in colour, don't you think? Sid's quite happy with black and white, too tight to pay the extra.'

The officer turned to Sid and shook his head despairingly. 'Indeed, madam. If I could just ask you a few questions about the night you found the body?'

Margaret began her uncontrollable jabbering again. 'Oh, terrible it was. So much blood, and to think if Sid and I weren't arguing, we wouldn't have found that poor man.'

The officer held up his hand. 'Madam, if I can stop you there. I understand that shortly before you found the body, you and your husband saw a man on the roof of this ballroom?'

Margaret drew a deep breath. 'Oh yes, we did. We didn't get a very good look at him though, did we, Sidney?'

By now, the henpecked Sid was ready to burst. 'Actually, officer, I got quite a good look at him. I couldn't really describe his face in any detail because he was silhouetted against a bright light behind him, but I could see he had a beard and he was wearing a long coat. He had something in his right hand which he was holding up high. It was a pole, probably about four feet long with something circular on one end.'

The detective pointed his torch at an object on the floor. 'Do you think it could have been this, sir?'

Sid stooped to look more closely at the object that PC Bardon had found earlier that day, illuminated in the torch beam. Sid scratched his head. 'Well, I couldn't be absolutely sure, but I would guess that it is. Is that blood?' Sid pointed to the circular emblem.

Margaret couldn't resist. 'Sidney, if this *was* an episode of *Softly, Softly*, you wouldn't be able to tell if that was blood. Not in black and white you wouldn't. Isn't that right, officer? I think we'll go back past the television rental place. Just have a look through the window.'

'Do you really think that if I had your stuff, I would keep it here, Masterton?'

Nathaniel Masterton rose from the chair on which he was sitting, his strength seemingly restored again. With one giant stride, he was standing inches from Craig Norton. 'Norton, don't mess me about. I know you have my stuff and I'm going to get it back and I don't care what I have to do to make it happen.'

Norton took a step backwards.

'You're mistaken, Masterton. That chest was passed down to Tara Jones. That makes it *her* property not yours.'

Masterton's anger was rising to boiling point. He lunged forward, and placing an ice-cold hand around Norton's throat, he squeezed, and pushed him against the wall.

'Norton, it's my fucking property. Just because she's family, it doesn't give her the right to hold on to what rightly belongs to The Brethren, and, more importantly, me. I *will* get my stuff back; my life depends on it and I will go to any lengths to get it!'

Letting go of Norton, Masterton turned to face his aunt and pointed a bony finger at her. 'You, Madame Volatska, are coming with me. Norton, you have twelve hours to give me my stuff back or you will be saying goodbye to Madame human chimney fucking Volatska forever.'

As Masterton paced slowly forwards to grab Mary's arm, the temperature in the room dropped. Between Masterton and Mary Sharp stood a girl. A girl from whom water dripped, whose soaking wet dress clung tightly to her body. Her hair was soaked and hanging limp over her shoulders.

Masterton was silent and just stared at the girl, his eyes becoming wide, he swallowed deeply and stepped back. 'No, no. Not you. No!'

In one massive stride, Masterton, having let go of Mary Sharp, was gone, the girl too. All that remained were two pools of water on the kitchen floor.

## Chapter 30

Tara Jones drove along the seafront, her attention to the road distracted by the sight of a sorry-looking police car against the seawall. By it stood a tall young constable. She pulled up against the kerb, reached over, wound down the passenger window and called out, 'Are you alright, officer?'

The young constable walked over and lowered his tall frame beside Tara's car. 'Thank you for stopping, miss. I'm fine. Reckon I'll have a stiff neck tomorrow morning though. Could you possibly do me a huge favour and somehow get in touch with the police station and let them know about my predicament? The radio in the vehicle has stopped working and I need to stay here to guard the scene.'

Tara smiled sweetly. 'I'll drive straight to the police station. I was rather hoping to catch up with Steve Bardon, to be honest. I'm sure help will be on its way very soon.'

With that, she waved a pretty hand, wound up the window and pulled away leaving a somewhat nervous Constable Murray alone with the very sorry-looking Morris.

Ten minutes later Tara pulled up outside Stonypool Police Station. Steve Bardon was climbing the steps that led to the front door. She wound down the window and called out, 'Hello gorgeous!'

The young constable took another step before turning. A big smile spread across his face and he ran back down the steps, crouching down beside Tara's car. He delivered a kiss on her pouting lips. 'Tara, just the person. Sorry to put business before pleasure, but can you come inside the station?'

Tara knew what this was about.

As they climbed the steps, Steve Bardon paused. 'We sent PC Murray out to see you. Did he take a statement?'

He pushed open the door of the police station and gestured for Tara to enter. As Bardon ushered her through the door, she delivered the bad news. 'Is PC Murray a tall man in a little Morris? If so, then I know why he didn't arrive.'

Bardon's forehead wrinkled inquisitively. 'Oh yes?'

Tara smiled cheekily. Bardon's heart fluttered.

'Yes, the car's embedded in the wall at the seafront. He's fine, but a little shaken, I would guess.'

'For goodness' sake! We'd better get down there, Tara. I'll just make a quick call to the workshop. They'll arrange a recovery truck. Our only other vehicle is out. Do you mind taking me in your car?' Tara's smile grew wider. Bardon's knees went weak.

'You can talk to me on the way down there, Steve.'

Seconds later they were pulling away from the police station.

'Tara, I understand from the desk sergeant that you telephoned earlier, saying that there was an intruder at the hotel and that he knew something about the missing baby?'

'Yes, I did, Steve. It was a Nathaniel Masterton, the same guy who turned up yesterday when you were out the back, and he said as much.' Tara placed a left hand on Bardon's right forearm after changing gear. The young constable blushed. Tara smiled. 'Well actually, Steve, it was more that he didn't deny Craig Norton's accusation.'

'Craig Norton was there?' Bardon's voice contained just a hint of jealousy.

'Yes Steve, and I'm very pleased he was. Craig seemed to know something about Masterton's intentions. Said something about page fifty-seven, whatever that means.'

Steve Bardon needed air. He wound down the passenger window a fraction. 'Seems that Mr Norton knows more than he's letting on. I think I need to talk to him again.' He wound down the window a little further, frowned and fell silent.

'Are you all right, Steve?' Tara had glanced round and seen the confused look on his face.

'Can you hear that, Tara?'

'Hear what, Steve?

97

'Pull over for a second.'

Tara pulled her car up against the kerb. The sound was now louder.

'An ice cream van's chimes!'

By now Tara could hear it too.

'But, Steve, we are at the seaside, in case you'd forgotten.' She smiled cheekily.

'Yes, but Tara, not only is it out of season, old Bill Berkley operated the only ice cream van in Stonypool. At least he did, until a month ago. Don't you remember … he died.'

Tara's pretty brow wrinkled in thought. 'Yes, Steve. I remember. I could hardly forget. They had the wake at my hotel in the function room. I was asked to provide soft ice cream and Cadbury Flakes. How could I forget?'

'Maybe it's someone lining up his patch for next season?'

The chimes, a repeating, weary music box version of 'Greensleeves' became ever louder.

'Look, Tara!'

Approaching them on the other side of the street was an ice cream van. As it came closer, Bardon's eyes widened.

'Shit!'

Tara turned sharply to look at Steve Bardon who just pointed straight ahead. The ice cream van was now nearly level with them. At the wheel, smiling broadly, sat Bill Berkley. A moment more and it had passed. Bardon turned his body in the seat to look behind.

As the ice cream van drove away from them, he saw below the rear window an emblem he knew. An inverted five-pointed star surrounded by a circle, with a reversed 'Z' at its centre, was now partially obscuring the Lyons Maid ice cream sticker with its happy, dancing children.

Tara selected first gear in her little Fiat and pulled away.

'That was just plain weird, Tara. A dead man driving an ice cream van! Mind you, nothing really surprises me lately.'

# Chapter 31

Rita Rawlson stood in front of the full-length wardrobe mirror in her bedroom. Her intention was to clear out Dennis' clothes from the other half of the wardrobe and bag them up to take to Oxfam. It was the first time in her life she'd ever thought of doing something charitable. However, she had become distracted when she tried on one of her old dresses that had been too small but now fitted. She posed and pouted.

Behind her, a voice said, 'Grow up, woman. Mutton dressed as lamb!'

Without turning, she knew to whom the voice belonged, but she had no choice but to turn.

Nathaniel Masterton sat upon the king-size bed, holding the jeans Rita had thrown there when she started trying on her old dresses. 'I'm surprised you can fit your ugly arse into these, woman!'

Rita's anger quickly boiled over. 'How the fuck did you get in here? More than that, what the fuck do you want?'

Masterton coughed, then waved a set of keys in front of her. 'I want you, Mrs Rita bloody Rawlson, and not in a sexual way. Perish the thought.' He coughed again and spat on the carpet.

'That's disgusting, you revolting pig! So what *do* you want then? Like I'd even consider sex with an old man like you!'

Masterton smiled. 'I don't consider one hundred and twenty years as old. I could have many more years if you do what I ask of you.'

Rita pulled down the hem of the dress she was wearing, realising a little too much leg was showing. 'Like I'd do anything for you, you bastard!'

'That's a bit strong, Rawlson. I can trace my lineage back to the early seventeenth century. I know who my parents are. Anyway, enough of your ranting, woman. You owe me. The last task I set you you failed miserably. I had to do it myself. Your next task you will not fail at, because if you do, you'll be meeting with your husband again rather sooner than you think.'

Rita closed the wardrobe door and took a couple of paces towards Masterton. 'Don't you threaten me, old man. You're lucky I haven't talked to the police about what you did to poor bloody Dennis.'

'I'll give you "poor bloody Dennis". You wanted him gone. In a couple of months, you'll be spending his life insurance and no doubt be under some tanned young foreigner abroad. You disgust me, woman, and if you don't do as I ask, you'll never get to spend that money, *or* feel the bed sheets of a luxury continental hotel under that fat arse of yours.'

Rita was trembling with rage. 'So, just what is it you want me to do?'

Masterton's coughing caused a pause in conversation. 'Madame Volatska. Know her?'

'Yes, of course. Everyone around here knows Mary.'

'Good. She has a nephew, Craig Norton.' Masterton again spat on the carpet. Rita felt bile rising in her throat. 'He's staying with her at the moment. He has something that belongs to me; a chest. I want you to get it back for me, or at the very least find out where he's hiding it. Use whatever means you can.' Masterton gave an exaggerated peal of laughter. 'Even your womanly charms if you have to!'

'And then you'll leave me alone?'

'Better than that, Mrs Rawlson. I may even reward you.'

Rita, distracted by the sound of an ice cream van's chimes right outside, turned towards the window. When she turned back, Masterton was gone.

Mary Sharp had poured herself a large gin with just a hint of tonic. The bottle had rattled against the rim of the glass as she poured. The events of the last few moments had left her shaking. 'Craig, what the bloody hell is going on?' She lit another cigarette.

'Sorry, Mary, excuse my language, but that bastard Masterton wants me to give him the chest that Tara Jones gave me to look after.'

Mary drew heavily on her cigarette. 'And ghost girl? Well, that's definitely what she is, isn't she, Craig?'

'Yes, but you don't seem that ruffled by the appearance of a ghost in your home.'

Mary blew out a cloud of blue smoke. 'It was a bit of a shock when I first saw her, of course, but I've seen ghosts before. Many are the times I've been invited to, or even held a séance.'

Craig smiled broadly. 'Well, my dear aunt, I can't tell you who the girl is, but you can certainly assist me with my plan to rid the town of this curse forever.'

PC Bardon carried on looking over his shoulder at the ice cream van, which was rapidly disappearing into the distance. Tara's car accelerated.

'Better get down the road and sort out PC Murray then, Steve.'

The young constable turned his head to face Tara. For a moment he was silent.

'Are you alright Steve?'

'I'm absolutely fine, Tara. It's just that you're so bloody gorgeous!' He leaned towards her and planted a kiss on her cheek. Tara giggled.

'Compliments like that can go to a girl's head, you handsome man!'

Steve Bardon smiled. As Tara accelerated, he turned to look forward. Something caught his attention.

'Look at that, Tara. Mutton dressed as lamb!'

Tara looked at the woman they were about to pass. Steve's description was certainly accurate, if not a little rude. Dressed in a short denim jacket over a flimsy blouse, a short skirt that revealed just a hint of suspender belt, hair piled high and with enough make-up to have decorated the faces of an entire group of dancing girls was a face Tara recognised.

'Bloody Rita Rawlson!' Tara grinned. 'It didn't take her long to get over her husband's death. On the pull, I reckon. Someone's going to be unlucky tonight!' She slowed the car as they passed, and waved.

A clearly embarrassed Rita lowered her gaze to the pavement and gave a short wave in return.

Outside the television rental shop that they passed shortly after, an elderly couple stood, the woman waving her finger at the man. *Married bliss*, Steve thought.

A few moments later, they were pulling up beside the sorry-looking Morris Panda car and an equally sorry-looking constable. Murray stood beside the damaged Morris that was partially blocking the pavement behind the seawall. He'd had eight offers of help, three 'oh dears' one 'are they making a film?' and so many peals of laughter he had lost count. He was sure help would arrive soon. After all, that nice young lady was going to let them know at the police station.

A horn sounded close by and he turned in the direction from which it had come. Pulling up by the kerb was a car in which sat that nice young lady and his colleague, Steve Bardon, who while trying to look serious was clearly trying very hard to suppress a grin.

Bardon wound down the passenger window of Tara's car and called out, 'Alright, Murray? Good idea for the pier next year that is ... bumper cars!' He could no longer hide his smirk as he clambered out of the car. 'What happened, Murray? Now take your time.' Bardon's smirk was now a full-on smile.

'An ice cream van. I was waiting to pull out of the road opposite, I looked both ways, pulled out, and the bloody thing was just there, like it appeared out of nowhere. If I had braked, it would have hit me. I don't like to think about the consequences of that. Anyway, I put my foot down and the car took off like a frightened rabbit and I collided with this wall. I was on my way to see a Miss Jones at the hotel. I hope someone's told her I'm going to be late. Thank goodness that lovely young lady stopped to help.'

Murray waved at Tara Jones, who cheekily blew him a kiss in return. The young constable quickly looked away.

'Well, Murray, Miss Jones knows the police were delayed, and I think she's guessed the reason.' Bardon put a hand on Murray's shoulder and walked him in the direction of Tara's car.

'PC Murray, may I introduce you to Tara Jones.'

Tara leaned across the passenger seat displaying a little too much cleavage for Bardon's liking, and offered a pretty hard through the window, which Murray shook gently.

'I was on my way to see you, Miss Jones, when, well, this happened. I understand you have information regarding the missing baby? Is there somewhere we can talk?'

The sound of a substantial diesel engine ended any chance of conversation for a few moments. The tow truck pulled up behind Tara's car and the driver shut down the engine. Tara got closer to the passenger window, revealing yet more cleavage. 'Well, if Steve, I mean PC Bardon, can supervise here, there's a cafe about a hundred yards away. I can leave the car here.'

Soon, Tara Jones and PC Murray were sitting at a table in Seashells Cafe.

Big Tony came over to the table and winked at Tara as he approached. 'Nice to see you, Tara. Another policeman? I thought you were seeing Steve Bardon?'

Big Tony smiled, PC Murray blushed, Tara laughed.

'News travels fast around here, Tony. That bit of gossip travelled faster than the gossip that "big" is not a word that should prefix your name.'

Big Tony let out a belly-laugh. 'Well, Tara, one day you might find out the truth, you little minx! What will it be, anyway?'

Over coffee, Tara told Murray about what had happened earlier at the hotel, while he busily took notes.

'You say page fifty-seven of a book? What book would that be?'

Tara took a sip of coffee, extracted a powder compact from her bag, opened it and pouted in the small round mirror. 'To be honest, Constable Murray, I'm not absolutely sure. You need to speak to Craig Norton about that.'

Murray wrote 'Craig Norton' in his notebook. 'And where would I find this Norton, Miss Jones?'

Tara clicked shut her powder compact. 'Most likely at his Aunt Mary's place. I'll give you the address.

Murray sipped his coffee. Big Tony gazed at Tara and smiled. Outside, a now silent ice cream van passed by.

## Chapter 32

Moira Taggart sat in her front room. The cup of tea she had made herself was cooling, the slice of Victoria sponge drying, and *"The Archers"* was on the radio as she dozed. There was a loud crackle from the radio. Moira awoke with a start. In front of her stood a young girl, her soaking wet white dress clinging to her body, her dark hair flat and stuck on her cheeks. Below her, two damp circles were forming upon the floor as water dripped from her white fingers. Moira let out a shriek. 'Who are you? What do you want?'

The radio continued to crackle. The girl turned slowly to her left and pointed to the bag that the spirit of a fisherman had given Moira at the museum. Moira stayed in her chair, her body rigid, goosebumps forming on her aged skin as the temperature in the room dropped. The girl knelt down by the bag and laid a hand upon its side then stood up. Moira knew she meant no harm.

'Young lady, you're dead, aren't you?'

The girl looked around then nodded.

'You poor thing. Can I help you?'

Moira's strange visitor lowered her head to look at the bag and brought her hands to her face, covering her eyes. Raising her head slowly she uncovered her eyes again, and for a few seconds just stared at Moira, pointed towards the bag, shook her head and faded away.

Craig Norton was arriving back at Mary Sharp's flat, having been to the newsagent's to buy a local paper, the headline of which read:

'MISSING BABY. HOPE RESTORED AS POLICE RECEIVE POSSIBLE LEAD.'

He wondered how the newspaper had received that information so fast, and from where, in time for the late edition of the paper.

Outside the flat stood a policeman, not PC Bardon but a very young constable whom Craig did not recognise.

'Mr Norton? Mr Craig Norton?' Murray walked towards an approaching Craig.

'Yes PC –?'

'Murray. PC Murray. I'm informed by a Miss Jones that you might be able to provide some detail regarding a book, an old man, and a missing baby?'

Craig tucked his newspaper under his arm and fumbled in his coat pocket for his keys. He ushered Murray into the kitchen and called out for his aunt. There was no answer. Showing the constable into the kitchen, he found a note on the table. He picked it up and read it:

*Craig*

*I've gone out for a couple of hours. The atmosphere in the flat is horrible. See you later.*

*Mary.*

'So how about you put the kettle on and tell me what you know, Mr Norton?'

Craig obliged, and over coffee he told Murray about the Brethren of the Visiting Spirits, Nathaniel Masterton and the significance of page fifty-seven of the book that he'd found in the chest that Tara had given him. 'So you see, Constable Murray, Masterton is trying to raise his former master and as I have told you, the sacrifice of a child under one year is critical to the ceremony. Masterton knows where that baby is, but what he doesn't know is where the chest is, and I would rather no one else knew either.'

At Seashells Cafe, a young enthusiastic journalist thanked Big Tony for his earlier phone call and information. He slipped a ten-shilling note into Tony's shirt pocket. The story had made it into the late edition of the local paper. Big Tony heard most of the local gossip during his working day.

Debbie Barry sat alone in her home. She had the strangest feeling, one of elation and hope. A feeling that made her believe her son was still alive. She smiled, something that she had not done since his disappearance.

Moira Taggart lay a towel over the two wet patches where the ghost girl had stood. She wanted to look inside the bag that the fisherman's spirit had given her, and that the girl had been so interested in, but knew she shouldn't.

Ken Lomes was sitting at a table in the saloon bar of the Ship and Anchor, reading again the invitation to his best friend's funeral. He shook his head and placed the little printed card down on the table in front of him.

Tara Jones and Steve Bardon were sitting together in the back room of the Beach View Hotel, watching the new BBC News and current affairs programme *Nationwide*. Tara turned off the table lamp by the sofa and sidled closer to the handsome young constable, her right hand had gradually worked its way up his left thigh and now rested in his crotch. Steve Bardon, his left arm, before, resting loosely around her shoulders, now pulled her close towards him. *Nationwide*'s Northern correspondent delivered a damning report on the state of hotels and guest houses in the Scarborough area.

Tara Jones pulled her lips away from Steve Bardon's for a moment, and in a low voice said, 'There's nothing wrong with my accommodation is there, Steve?'

He smiled and placed his lips back upon hers.

# Chapter 33

Nathaniel Masterton stood in the middle of the dance floor of the old Empire Ballroom, arms stretched wide, a blue almost purple glow surrounding him. Outside, above the ballroom, the same glow had formed over the roof. Masterton chanted a strange incantation and then cursed Rita Rawlson. 'Rawlson, your time is running out. I will do it myself!'

There was a rumble that sounded like thumber but wasn't. The floor shook. Outside the front doors, Frank Chapley, clad in the white sheet from the morgue, stood cursing Nathaniel Masterton.


PC Murray had put the final full stop on the statement he had taken from Craig Norton. What he had heard during the past half hour had been difficult for the young constable to digest.

As Norton showed him to the front door of the flat, he said, 'Thank you, Mr Norton. If you think of anything else, give me a call at the station.'

From the pavement opposite the front of the flat came a call.

'Craig!' An underdressed and overly made-up Rita Rawlson began walking over, passing a smirking Constable Murray on her way. 'You're Craig, yes? Is Mary in? We haven't been introduced properly. I'm Rita Rawlson. You undoubtedly know about my husband, Dennis, and his unexpected and tragic death? I've called to see your aunt.'

Rita unbuttoned her jacket and pulled at the hem of her top, increasing the amount of ample cleavage on display. Craig averted his gaze.

'I'm sorry, Rita. She's out at the moment. I've no idea when she'll be back.' Rita was already through the front door before Craig could put up any resistance.

'I'll come in and wait if that's alright with you, Craig?'

As Rita made her bottom-shaking way to the kitchen, Craig muttered under his breath, 'You haven't given me much choice, Mrs Rawlson.'

'Sid! Sid! Come here!'

The elderly couple who had found Dennis Rawlson's body were spending the day at home after their new colour television had been delivered that morning. Margaret had even kept it on for the period of the trade test transmission, although much of the day had been consumed by nagging her henpecked husband and congratulating herself on having rented her pride and joy, the colour television that was now displaying the first of the day's programmes, a round up of national news.

Margaret called out for her husband again. 'Sid, come here now!' Sid sighed deeply, put his newspaper down on the kitchen table and made his way to the living room and his nagging wife. 'There's going to be a news feature on Stonypool, because of all the strange things that have been going on.'

Sid was now interested and settled himself on the sofa next to his unusually silent wife. For the first time in many months the usually quiet Sid became excited. The news feature had moved from the seafront to the old Empire Ballroom. It was filmed during late evening and required the use of bright lighting. The camera panned upwards to the roof where a dull but distinct blue almost purple glow could be seen. The fact it would not have been discernible on a black and white television was not lost on him. The camera panned down from the roof and settled on a view of the side alley to the right of the ballroom.

'Margaret, look at that!'

Just turning the corner to enter the side alley from the right was a man in a long coat, sporting a neatly trimmed beard and long hair, pushing a wheelchair in which sat the man whose body Sid and Margaret had found behind the ballroom. The man pushing the wheelchair turned momentarily to look at the camera. The bright lights reflected off a silver chain around the man's neck. From the chain hung a medallion, an inverted five-pointed star surrounded by a circle, in its centre a reversed 'Z'.

Margaret, eyes fixed on the television, slapped her husband on his right knee.

'Well, Sid, I don't think you would have spotted all that on our old television. In fact, it wouldn't even have been on at this time of day. I think you'd better pop down to the phone box and call the police. Oh, and while you're down there, you can pick me up some chocolate from the shop to celebrate!'

For once, Sid couldn't argue with what Margaret had said – apart from the chocolate. It was he who had spotted the man and the wheelchair; it was he who should be celebrating with a treat. Then it struck him that his wife was actually wanting to celebrate the arrival of the colour television.

'Coffee, Rita?' Craig Norton was already suspicious of Rita Rawlson's motives.

She didn't seem to know his aunt that well, and conversation soon dried up. Craig stood, and when his back was turned, Rita undid another button on her blouse, revealing a hint of lacy bra underneath. Then she hitched up her skirt to the top of her stockings and shifted the chair upon which she was sitting from beneath the table. Craig returned from the sink with the two mugs of coffee. Presented with the sight of a partially exposed Rita, he stood motionless.

'Come on, Craig. Come and sit with Rita.' Nervously, Craig edged his way towards the table. Rita hitched her skirt just a little higher. 'Craig, a friend of mine has told me you have something that belongs to him.' Craig put the coffee on the table. Rita attempted a seductive smile. 'And I have something for you if you tell me where it is.' She hitched her skirt even higher.

'Rita, I knew you hadn't come here to see my aunt. Your friend, although believe me, he is no friend, and believe me I know to whom you are referring, is completely deluded if he thinks that sending you here offering me sexual favours is going to work.'

Rita reached out and grabbed Craig's hand, pulling him towards her. He stumbled and fell into her lap. Rita screamed, stood up and sent Craig scrabbling to the ground. Looking up from the floor by the sink, just a few feet away, stood the drenched girl, water dripping from her hands and onto the floor. Her face was as white as bone china and her eyes were fixed on Rita. Pulling her skirt hem down, she ran to the front door, stumbling as she went.

The front door slammed. Rita was gone. The girl slowly faded.


# Chapter 34

Mary Sharp was sitting at a circular table at a friend's house. The curtains were drawn and the lights were out. Mary was much more Madame Volatska than Mrs Sharp right now.

Her best friend, Vera Binds, called for silence among the assembled ladies. Vera had long considered herself as being a medium of some considerable ability, and indeed her occasional afternoon séances had confirmed this. Today's séance was to be very different.

Vera closed her eyes and breathed heavily. 'Ladies, if we could remain totally silent and all join hands, I shall attempt communication with the spirit world.'

The air in the room was still, the only sound Vera's steady breathing. The silence was broken by her distinctive séance voice.

'I call upon those around us who are now in spirit to elect one who can represent you all.'

For a minute the silence returned, then there was a shuffling sound from the corner of the room.

'Thank you. It's good to have you with us. Can I ask your name?' Vera's voice had dropped an octave and she breathed heavily.

'My name is Arthur Rowan. I speak on behalf of those who surround me.'

Vera's voice returned to normal. 'Can I ask who is with you?' Her voice dropped an octave again.

'Those that are gathered here with me are not at peace; they are angry.'

The table shook. There was the sound of footsteps upon the wooden floor surrounding the gathering. The sound became louder, and Vera Binds' voice became her own again.

'I'm so sorry to hear that, Arthur. Can you tell me why it is they are angry?'

The sound of footsteps upon the floor became much louder, the air became icy cold. Vera groaned, and as she did, the groan became steadily lower in tone, and louder, until the room seemed to reverberate. Then she brought a fist down heavily upon the table, and in a strange, low voice said, 'Please tell me, Arthur.'

The voice that answered came not from Vera, but from elsewhere within the room.

'Because he killed us fifty years ago! Fifty years we have followed him, awaiting the moment to take our revenge! Now that opportunity is fast approaching. Many who perished are unaware that they died. They are gathering within the town, expecting to see what they came for fifty years ago. We seek revenge for them too.'

The sound of footsteps became louder still, as if a crowd was agitated and on the move as one. The air became colder still. There was a blinding flash that revealed a cloud of vapour, the visible breath of those gathered at the table. But more than that, it revealed a crowd of some twenty figures: men in overcoats, some with caps, ladies in long dresses sporting winter jackets and hats.

The room was dark once again. The ladies' eyes were not accustomed to the dark after that bright flash. Mary Sharp raised herself from the chair upon which she had been sitting and stumbled towards the door behind her, beside which the light switch was positioned.

A moment later, the room was illuminated by the shaded light bulb at its centre. The ghostly crowd was gone. Vera Binds sat slumped in her chair, mouth open wide, staring fixedly at the ceiling.


# Chapter 35

Nathaniel Masterton was beyond angry. Outside the old Empire Ballroom, night had encroached. For a while he stood on the steps at the front of the ballroom. From a pocket in his long leather coat he drew a knife, which glinted in the lights of the promenade. He muttered under his breath, 'Fuck you, Rita Rawlson. Your time is fast running out.' He then coughed violently and fell to his knees, reminding him that *his* time was also running out.

On the road in front of him a Morris 1100 Panda car pulled up, in which sat PC Murray. Murray carefully applied the handbrake, and, stopping the engine, memories of what had happened to that other unfortunate Morris came into his mind. The sight of a grown man on his knees outside the ballroom had raised Murray's curiosity. Grabbing a torch from the parcel shelf, he opened the driver's door, stepped out, and made his way towards the kneeling figure. 'Hello, sir. Can I help you?'

Masterton turned his head to face the dazzling beam of the torch. Covering his eyes with his left hand, he struck out with his right, knocking the torch out of Murray's hand and sending it rolling down the concrete steps. But Murray had, in those few seconds of light, remembered the description of Nathaniel Masterton he had been given.

'Masterton? It *is* Nathaniel Masterton, isn't it? We've been looking for you in connection with the disappearance of a baby and a suspicious death. My name is PC Murray. If you would like to accompany me to the car, we can discuss it at the local police station.'

By now, Masterton had raised himself to his full height. For a moment, Murray thought Masterson was going to comply with his request, but in one slick movement the evil man had taken the knife from his pocket and held it against Murray's throat.

'Listen to me, bluebottle, fuck off now or I'll be implicated in another death: yours!' Masterton's eyes became fixed on something behind Murray. He dropped the knife to his waist. Murray grabbed Masterton's arm and twisted it behind his back, turning in the process. Approaching, a short distance away, was a small crowd, a crowd comprising men in overcoats – some with caps – and women in long dresses, winter jackets – some with hats.

As they drew closer, Masterton's features became frozen and he ceased to struggle against Murray's grasp, and in a low voice said, 'Constable Murray, take me to your car.'

Craig Norton sat at the bar of the Ship and Anchor, being served by a very dejected Ken Lomes.

'I can't believe he's gone. Poor Dennis. Got the funeral to get through yet.'

Craig gave Ken a sympathetic look. 'Yes, horrible. The police are treating his death as suspicious.'

Ken sighed. 'Ultimately, whatever the circumstances, I blame his wife, Rita.'

Craig wasn't sure whether he should mention his encounter with the widow Rawlson, but, gathering Ken Lomes was not her greatest fan, he felt he had nothing to lose. 'Rita Rawlson came to visit me. She came at the request of a Nathaniel Masterton. Tried to seduce me to gain some information.'

Ken became more attentive. 'Masterton? He's that weird guy with the long hair and leather coat who keeps springing up out of nowhere, isn't he? What possible interest could he have in Rita the Cheater, or maybe that's the reason: sexual gratification.'

Craig smiled. 'Maybe, but I think he's more interested in something that belongs to him, that he believes I am in possession of. If you're looking for the person responsible for your friend's death, I would look no further than that evil bastard.'

Ken was distracted. 'Listen. Can you hear that?'

Craig frowned. 'Hear what, Ken?

For a moment, Ken was silent, clearly straining to hear. 'It's a bloody ice cream van!'

PC Murray was somewhat surprised by how Masterton had given himself up so easily. Sitting in the back of the Panda car, Masterton was silent. Murray glanced at him in the rear-view mirror. Masterton was beginning a smile that quickly became broad. Murray's attention was shifted from the mirror to the road ahead. Approaching on his side of the road was an ice cream van. Murray shouted, 'Shit!'

Masterton, hand on the door handle, called out, 'Goodbye, bluebottle!'

As Murray braked heavily, Masterton pulled on the door handle and as the door swung open, threw himself out into the road. Murray pulled sharply to the left on the Panda car's steering wheel, causing him to swerve towards the kerb and a seafront seating kiosk. With a crunch of twisting metal and rain of shattering glass, the kiosk collapsed, the car coming to rest on top of the debris. For a moment Murray sat watching steam rise from beneath the crumpled bonnet. Feeling somewhat nauseous, he wound down the driver's door window for air. Fading into the distance he heard the ice cream van's chimes: an unfamiliar tune. *Wagner again*, he thought.

## Chapter 36

Big Tony had locked up Seashells Cafe for another day. Pulling the collar of his coat up against the chill of the stiff evening breeze, he put his keys in his pocket and turned to his left to start his walk home. His attention was immediately taken by the unusual crowd gathered outside the old Empire Ballroom. Men in overcoats, some with caps, women in long dresses with winter jackets, and some with hats. One thing Big Tony knew for sure is that they were not dressed in the current fashion, and of course he knew for sure that they certainly weren't gathering for an event at the ballroom. Walking towards the crowd, Tony called out, 'Nothing on there tonight, people. Hasn't been for years.'

The entire crowd turned to face him. Tony's blood ran cold. Their faces were shades of red, mottled, distorted, burned. White eyes stared out from the seared flesh. Big Tony took a deep gulp of the cold evening air and ran in the opposite direction. Within a couple of minutes, he stumbled breathless into the public bar of the Ship and Anchor. 'Whisky! Give me a whisky now!'

Ken Lomes grabbed a tumbler from behind the bar and thrust it under a whisky optic.

Big Tony pulled a barstool towards him and sat down heavily. 'Norton! Thank fuck you're here! There's some really weird shit going on tonight!' He swallowed his whisky in a single gulp. 'Come on, Norton. Come and take a look!'

Grabbing Norton's arm, Big Tony pulled him towards the door of the saloon bar, barstool toppling behind him.

Mary Sharp was still surprised and somewhat shaken by the outcome of the séance earlier that day. It had taken her a good half an hour to bring her friend Vera Binds round from the deep trance she had entered. In fact, she hadn't like to leave her, and had stayed on at her house for a while following her recovery. When Vera had assured her that she was alright, after some dispute, she had left to clear her head. Mary had decided to walk home along the seafront.

On passing the Ship and Anchor, she was stopped in her tracks by her nephew being dragged out through the saloon bar door by Big Tony. The sight made her smile. 'Everything alright, Craig?'

Craig Norton had started to reply when Big Tony cut him short.

'Crazy shit ma'am. Crazy! Thought Norton here ought to see it. The dead are gathering at the old ballroom for a show that isn't going to happen! I reckon they're dead anyway. That's why I thought Norton here should take a look.'

By now Big Tony had let go of Craig Norton's arm.

Mary's nephew was able to get a word in. 'Mary, if what he says is true, I really think you should join us.'

Big Tony waved his arms as if to usher them on. 'True? Of course it's bloody true. Excuse my language, ma'am. I saw them with my own eyes.'

The trio marched purposefully along the seafront in the direction of the old Empire Ballroom.

PC Murray stood surveying the destruction caused by his Panda car. He knew it was the same ice cream van that had caused both his first and second accident within the same week, but how was he going to explain this to his superiors?

The radio in the damaged Panda car came to life. 'Panda one from control.'

Murray reached through the open driver's window and grabbed the microphone. 'Panda one receiving.'

'Panda one, your location please?'

'Control, seafront opposite Preston Road.'

'Panda one, we've had reports of a crowd gathered outside the old Empire Ballroom. Can you attend please?'

Murray paused trying to think of an answer. 'Control from Panda one. Negative. Got a bit of car trouble. Can you arrange a breakdown truck please?' He then put his head back in through the driver's window and replaced the microphone in its clip. He tilted his head to look through the windscreen.

In front of the car stood Masterton, grinning wildly.

Tara Jones left the Beach View Hotel in the charge of her able assistant, Linda. With only two guests in residence, and as both had dined out that evening, she had absolutely no doubt about Linda's ability to cope. Outside the hotel, Steve Bardon stood waiting.

'Good evening, gorgeous! I thought we could start the evening with a drink at the Ship and Anchor and decide where to go from there.'

Tara threw her arms around the young constable and pushed her body tight against his. She whispered in his ear, 'I know what *I* want to do later, constable!'

Steve smiled broadly.

Ten minutes later the handsome couple were sitting together in the saloon bar of the Ship and Anchor, drinks in front of them. There was only one other customer, who was in the public bar.

Ken Lomes, glass and cloth in hand, wandered over to their table. 'Good evening, Tara, Constable Bardon.'

Bardon pulled out a chair and beckoned for Ken to sit down. 'Ken, how are you? I still can't believe what happened to Dennis.'

Ken placed the glass and cloth on the table. 'I can't stop thinking about it. It's his funeral I'm dreading. I can't look Rita in the eye. I know I should make allowances, but she progressively ruined his life.'

Steve Bardon looked at Ken and shook his head. Ken was unaware of the game of footsie taking place underneath the table. 'Very bad business, Ken. Very bad indeed. We're still treating his death as suspicious, but the body was released to the undertaker after the post mortem. I'll keep you posted on developments.'

Ken thanked him. 'Yeah, already got an invitation to the funeral. Rita didn't hang about arranging that.'

Of course, Bardon knew all about the recent involvement of the CID and the subsequent forensic investigation around the object found at the old Empire Ballroom.

Ken turned to face Tara, who had slid a hand under the table and was squeezing Bardon's right knee. 'Had a friend of yours in earlier, Tara, that Craig Norton guy. He got dragged out by Big Tony, literally. Something about crazy shit going on Tony said, excuse my language.' Bardon giggled as Tara moved her hand round and tickled the back of his knee. Ken frowned. 'No honestly, PC Bardon, I know it sounds funny, but Big Tony seemed genuinely concerned.'

Bardon slipped an arm under the table, moved Tara's hand and squeezed it tightly. 'Any idea what direction they were heading, Ken?'

'I think they turned right out of here. I saw them pass the window.'

Steve Bardon stood, drank the rest of his pint in one gulp and slipped on his jacket. 'Come on, Tara. I think we'd better take a look at this.'

Tara tutted sarcastically. 'You mean *you'd* better take a look at this. Ever the policeman!'

A moment later, Ken was once again alone with his one remaining customer, who despite ordering half a pint of bitter had not drunk a drop of it. Ken attempted to make conversation with him. 'Cold out there tonight, mate.'

The man raised his head and fixed Ken in his stare. Ken looked into his eyes, which seemed somehow glassy and lifeless. He couldn't help but notice what looked like recent scarring covering much of the right side of his face. A glimmer of a smile came to the man's face, the action of which, combined with the heavy scarring around his right eye, caused the eye to close completely in some grotesque wink. Ken shivered.

'Not for me it's not, mate. Glad to be out of the heat.'

Ken returned to his position behind the bar, avoiding any further eye contact with the strange customer. He turned to examine the optics. When he turned back again, his only customer was gone, his drink untouched.

Outside the Ship and Anchor, Steve Bardon and Tara Jones now stood hand in hand. Tara kissed Steve on the cheek but Steve was distracted as a tow truck passed by. 'That's not good, Tara.'

Tara frowned. 'What's not good, Steve?'

'That was the tow truck from the force vehicle workshop. Murray's on tonight. I really hope he's not had another disaster!'

Tara laughed, something that now never failed to melt the young constable's heart. 'Come on, Steve. Let's go and see what Big Tony is on about.'


# Chapter 37

The sun had set some hours ago. A chill breeze blew along the promenade from the west, the direction in which Steve and Tara were walking. In the distance, the chimes of an ice cream van were steadily becoming louder. The couple carried on walking. Coming towards them along the promenade was that very ice cream van, displaying just side lights. It performed a U-turn and pulled up next to them. The passenger window lowered. Masterton who was occupying the seat turned to face them.

'Bardon, you'd better get down the road. Your boy has had a mishap!' Before Bardon could answer, the ice cream van pulled away, Masterton's laughter standing out clearly above the chimes.

'I knew it, Tara. I just knew it. Bloody Murray!'

The couple started walking again with a little more urgency. It was where the promenade curved slightly that they were afforded a clear view ahead. In the middle distance they could see the old Empire Ballroom. Outside, a crowd had gathered. Above the ballroom a blue almost purple glow swirled like paint in water. Bardon took Tara's hand.

'That's bizarre Tara! Who are those people?'

Tara squeezed his hand tightly. 'I really don't like it, Steve. Whatever is that glow, too? If the place was still open, I would have said it was some kind of lighting effect, but the place has been closed for years. And what are all those people hanging about for?'

Steve Bardon placed an arm around Tara's shoulder and pulled her towards him. 'Well, come with me and we may well find out!'

Outside the old Empire Ballroom, the strange crowd milled about restlessly. Big Tony, Craig Norton, and Mary Sharp stood on the other side of the promenade, watching.

Big Tony slapped Craig's back. 'See, like I said. Crazy shit man!'

Mary seemed transfixed by the unusual appearance of the gathered men and women. 'I have to say, Craig, Tony's right. This is crazy. Probably crazier than you think. I attended a séance at Vera Binds' place today, and the place became filled with those characters–although nowhere near as many as there are now. They said *he* had killed them fifty years ago.'

Craig knew who these people were and he knew he had to enact his plan soon.

Nathaniel Masterton sat on a bench looking out to sea. He was becoming weaker by the hour. If he did not raise his Master, the time he had been granted would soon be over. So what if the people of the town suffered at his hands? So what if a baby died? It did not yet know what life really was anyway. But *he* had well over one hundred years of memories. After all, he had killed many times now and had no regrets. He knew now that he would struggle to defend himself from the spirits of those whose lives he had taken.

Simon Clark-Mathos had taken him under his wing when the Brethren of the Visiting Spirits was just a small group of privileged male youths who took an interest in the occult. Mathos had believed that by calling up the spirits of the dead, he could gain knowledge and power beyond any other. It seemed his idea was indeed valid. When he started The Brethren, Clark-Mathos was a weak and sickly youth. At the time of his death, he was a man of strength, both bodily and mentally, a man who had a following around the country. And in the company of his dedicated group of friends he would tour theatres and halls where followers and intrigued onlookers alike would gather to watch as he proved time and time again that he could summon entities from the spirit world. That through contact with them he was able to perform feats of superhuman ability.

His belief in his powers became stronger. Masterton had been granted the power of an extended life in return for his help and dedication to the Brethren. Together, they believed they could become immortal. Masterton was already an old man when he had become involved with Clark-Mathos. He had everything to gain by his association with the charismatic youth: strength, wealth and many more years of life maybe?

Clark-Mathos had come to believe that he could bring a corpse back from the dead. Such was his dedication to his master, Masterton, a man who up until then had led a gracious and respected life, became nothing short of a brutal killer, to provide corpses upon which his master could trial his techniques. Eventually, Clark-Mathos believed he had perfected a ritual that would work, but that required the taking of a young girl's life, whose mortal remains would form an essential part of the ritual, a girl he had tasked Masterton with finding. A ritual for which nearly all the essential components were contained within the chest that Craig Norton had taken and hidden. A ritual that Clark-Mathos had fettled and developed until he believed that it could, with the addition of the sacrificial offering of a pure and innocent soul, a baby, raise the Master of all darkness.

The rituals were written down and published in a book, of which fewer than one hundred copies were ever printed. Now considered a fascinating and valued treasure by followers of the occult, Masterton's own copy was within that chest, the chest that contained everything needed to bring back his own Master of Darkness, Clark-Mathos, to grant an extension of his life. For he knew that Clark-Mathos was dead or, as he preferred to believe, in a resting state until summoned.

Fifty years ago, at a gathering at the Empire Ballroom in Stonypool, Clark-Mathos had intended to provide those gathered with a dramatic spectacle. He would raise a spirit, a force, an entity so evil that he would gain the respect of thousands if not hundreds of thousands. But that night had not gone to plan. The ritual was well in progress. Above the ballroom a strange blue almost purple light had formed which grew brighter with every passing minute. There had been a storm, lightning, A fire had begun within the structure of the roof.

He, Masterton, had looked up from the stage and seen it spreading. He should have called a halt to the proceedings and raised the alarm, but the lives of others meant nothing to him now. The alarm was finally raised when a woman, her dress on fire, jumped from the balcony onto the crowd below. In the screaming, crying, shouting confusion, many of the gathered crowd perished as those on the balcony continued to leap onto those below, some with their clothes aflame.

Clark-Mathos had escaped unseen through the rear entrance of the ballroom, leaving behind the chest into which his then girlfriend had repacked its contents and fled in the same direction as her faithless boyfriend. As he fled, he had cursed the town and its people, something he had planned to do since his dispute with the town council. After all, his reign of power was now over. He knew he could never recover from this. He fled abroad until he considered it safe to return to England, an England where he still had some dedicated followers. People, who maybe could help him re-form the Brethren.

The organisation continued for another five years, its numbers dwindling. Of course, he had continued to dabble in the dark arts and it's likely that this is how he met his end, for he was found dead in a room of a cheap London boarding house, his eyes wide open and a look of absolute terror upon his face, his clothes partially torn from his body and upon his bare chest, deep wounds that looked as though they had been inflicted by claws. The wall behind his head was scorched, appearing as if a flame had played upon it.

Masterton, from that point, knew his lifespan was almost certainly limited. When granted his life extension, it had been on the understanding that he would continue to support the cause of the Brethren and assist Clark-Mathos. And if he proved worthy, his life would be extended again. But with his master gone, how could this be? Masterton needed to raise his master and prove himself worthy of another life extension, and the few days during which the curse on this town would take place provided that opportunity. But he needed that chest in which was contained all he would need to execute his plan. From within his coat, he took out his knife, which glinted in the orange glow of the sodium street light above him. Rita Rawlson had one more chance, or she would be a dead woman for sure.

The sound of a seagull's screeching call broke Masterton's chain of thought. Looking up from the bench on which he was sitting, in the poor light he could see a group of people walking towards him. As the group became more defined under a street light some twenty yards away, he could see that they were men clothed in overcoats, some with caps, but all had one feature in common: their faces were horribly disfigured. He rose from the bench, his legs weak, his body heavy, his energy yet more depleted. Coughing, he inhaled air deep into his ancient lungs and shouted out, 'Fuck off! Leave me alone!'

# Chapter 38

Big Tony, Craig Norton, Mary Sharp, and the in-love couple, Steve Bardon and Tara Jones, stood on the opposite side of the road, facing the old Empire Ballroom. All eyes were trained upon the strange crowd as they milled about upon the steps of the once grand venue.

Big Tony squeezed Craig Norton's shoulder. 'Who are these weirdos? What do they want?'

Craig Norton shook his head. 'If I was to tell you, Tony, you wouldn't believe me. Like you say, crazy shit!'

Tara Jones raised a hand to her pretty nose. 'What *is* that smell? It's like a burnt joint of meat.'

Steve Bardon squeezed her other hand tightly, and as he did, several members of the crowd turned to face them.

Bardon turned his head towards Tara. 'I think that's your explanation. Look at their faces!'

Tara gagged and turned away.

Big Tony was now standing next to Mary Sharp. 'This shit is getting even crazier. Look!'

At the front of the crowd, which was now forming into an orderly queue, a tall grotesquely deformed man was shaking the locked ballroom doors. From behind the grime-encrusted glass came a circle of light that gradually grew smaller as a man in a brown warehouse coat drew closer, his torch scanning left and right. With a rattling of chain and a turning of locks, one door partially opened and a voice called out, 'Go away. It's not until tomorrow. You know that!'

The orderly crowd broke down into a disorderly mob again, then slowly they dispersed, some heading east and some west along the promenade, some heading towards the beach and some towards the town.

Craig Norton stood behind his aunt. 'Mary, I'm going to need your help – and soon. I have a feeling the town could be in for a bad night.'

From a distance, through the poorly lit night they heard a man call out, 'Fuck off. You're dead! Leave me alone!'

Craig Norton placed a hand on his aunt's back and frowned. Yes, tonight would be bad, but tomorrow he would enact his plan. However, there were still many hours to get through though.

By nine o'clock the town's streets were relatively quiet. The Empire Ballroom, that sentinel of the town's past, stood deserted, silent, brooding, like some gigantic creature from mythology that had slipped into an unsettled slumber from which it might awake angrily at any moment. The aftermath of PC Murray's mishap had been cleared away. The young policeman was now patrolling the town on foot, tilting his head from side to side, knowing that his neck was gradually stiffening from the whiplash he had experienced earlier. In the distance he heard a scream, although it was impossible to tell exactly from which direction it had come. He only knew, as he stood on the promenade looking out to sea, that it had come from behind him.

As he turned to face in the opposite direction, from a matter of a few yards away, he heard a man groan agonisingly, then from the same direction someone ran out from the shadows beneath the buildings opposite. In the glow of the streetlights Murray saw the glint of metal. A knife? But then, whoever it was, was gone. Something fell from the sky, narrowly missing the surprised constable as it did so. He looked down at the pavement where it had fallen. A seagull lay twitching, blood from its neck flowing from where its head should have been. Murray gagged and then, with one stroke of his policeman's boot, kicked the now motionless corpse against the seawall. No sooner had he done so than another, then another mutilated corpse fell nearby. Turning around, many were falling, forcing him to run for the shelter offered by the arch of the pier entrance. From behind him came the sound of birds calling, and the thump, thump as dead seagulls fell upon the pier decking. Only the calls weren't those of seagulls, but those of crows cawing. For a moment one of the jet-black birds barely visible against the night sky flew past on the other side of the pier gates. Murray may not have noticed it if it had not been for the whiteness of the seagull that hung, wings outstretched, its neck held in the crow's beak.

He heard the sound of running steps heading away from him along the pier, then when they had stopped, a splash. Among the falling and fallen gulls, Murray made a dash towards a seaside shelter where he slumped heavily onto a bench, brushing feathers from the shoulders of his tunic. Focusing on the pier head, he could see clearly in the strange blue almost purple glow that hung there, hundreds of the black birds silhouetted, wheeling, cawing and beneath the seagulls falling on the pier and into the sea below. He thought he heard a man's voice call his name.

## Chapter 39

Moira Taggart had fallen asleep in her front room with the radio turned on. The programme to which she had been listening had long finished, and some light music was now playing, fading leaving just a weak and occasional crackle. The bag the ghostly fisherman had given her sat against the opposite wall, shaking and rattling. The crackling from the radio now faded almost to nothing but then, from its speaker came the shout of a girl's voice.

'Moira!'

Moira awoke with a start, reached out, switched on the table lamp beside her, but in the same moment sent it crashing to the floor. Raising her old and aching body from the chair, she made her stumbling, unsteady way across the room towards the door, by which was the light switch. The radio crackled, the bag against the opposite wall rattled and tipped over. Moira flicked the light switch. For a moment, the room filled with light that grew steadily brighter until there was a loud pop, then darkness and the sound of fragments of the shattered light bulb raining down. The crackling from the radio increased and formed into words, a girl's voice.

'Moira, you must help me. There is a man called Norton. Take the bag to him.'

Debbie Barry sat on her bed, her spirit crushed, that former rush of hope now gone. She was now sure she would never see her son again. On the bedside cabinet was a picture of the missing child. A tear formed and rolled down her cheek to be followed by another and another. She lay down upon the bed, sobbing uncontrollably.

In the room next door, the empty cot began to shake. Something moved beneath the covers, something that writhed and whimpered. Outside, under the orange glow of a streetlight stood Frank Chapley, his mortuary sheet billowing in the gentle breeze, his eyes fixed upon Debbie Barry's house.

At the Ship and Anchor Ken Lomes was awoken by the sound of glasses smashing downstairs. Dozy from sleep, it took a few moments for the sound to register. Rising from his bed, he pulled on his trousers and made his way out to the landing and, after pausing momentarily, continued his way slowly down the staircase, every step measured and gentle so as to make the minimum of noise. At the foot of the stairs, he picked up his snooker cue, holding it with the grip uppermost. The sound of glasses breaking came from behind the door that led to the public bar. Ken placed his left hand upon the doorknob and gently rotated it until the latch was clear. Then, in one swift movement, he pushed open the door.

In front of him, barely visible in the darkness was a figure, back towards him, right arm raised. A pint glass fell from its hand. Ken swung the snooker cue, stumbling as it passed straight through the figure, which turned slowly to face him. It was the strange customer who had been the only customer in the bar for a while earlier that day. He stared fixedly at Ken from half-closed eyes set deep in his burnt face. The distorted lips parted.

'Where is it? Where are you hiding it?'

Ken guessed to what his ghostly visitor was referring. The previous day, after his strange customer had left, Ken had picked up a small gold medallion from the floor of the bar: a symbol, an inverted five-pointed star surrounded by a circle, in its centre a reversed 'Z'. Turning around, Ken pressed the SALE button on the till, and from one of the compartments in the cash drawer he took the medallion, turned back to face his uninvited guest, and held it out at arm's length.

An ice-cold hand touched his as the medallion was taken by its owner, whose ghastly smile twisted the hideous burnt face, from the lips of which came the words, 'Thank you. Sorry about the mess!'

Then he was gone, leaving Ken standing alone amidst the broken glass.

At the Beach View Hotel, Steve Bardon and Tara Jones were together in bed. Steve had fallen into a deep and contented sleep. Tara was sitting up, propped awake against her pillows, with a satisfied smile upon her face. From the corridor outside her accommodation, she heard footsteps, but there were only two guests staying at the hotel and they were staying on the first floor with absolutely no reason to ascend to the third. She shook the young constable by the shoulder and called out his name, 'Steve, Steve!'

Steve Bardon awoke with a start. 'What? What's the matter?'

'Steve, there's someone in the corridor. I can hear footsteps.'

'Tara, it's probably just those guests.'

'But why would they come up here, Steve?'

'Probably just being nosey.'

'Take a look will you, Steve. Please.'

Pulling on his trousers, Steve Bardon rose from the bed where minutes before he had been peacefully dreaming, despite his concerns earlier in the evening regarding PC Murray's ability to deal with whatever may arise after a troubled evening. Somewhat reluctantly, the barefooted Bardon made his way out to the hallway and along to the front door of Tara's accommodation. For a moment he stood still, just listening. There were no footsteps to be heard, although he knew he should check the corridor just to put Tara's mind at rest. He unlatched the door and unclipped the flimsy safety chain. He would have to have a word with Tara about her safety. Opening the door, he took a step forward and turned his head to the right to look along the corridor that was always kept lit at night. Seeing no one, he turned his head to the left.

He recoiled with shock and leaned heavily against the open door for support, causing it to crash noisily against the wall. He stared with revulsion at what stood just a few feet away in the corridor. A woman, her body covered by a nightdress down to her knees, long dark lank hair framing a face as white as paper, her eyes rotated upwards in their sockets, the skin around them dark and discoloured. Her arms hung at her sides and from the right wrist blood trickled down her open palm to drip off the middle two fingers.

The noise of the door crashing against the wall had attracted Tara's attention and within seconds, a dressing gown pulled loosely around her body, she was at Steve's side, her eyes fixed upon the ghastly vision from which Steve could not avert his gaze. The level-headed landlady pulled Steve Bardon back until he was no longer able to see what had caused him to lose all power of bodily motion. He sat down heavily on a chair in the hallway to which Tara directed him. With one swift movement, she slammed the front door.

Steve struggled for words. 'W-w-what just happened? Was she real?'

Tara stood in front of him and placed a reassuring hand on his right shoulder. 'Er ...well, I hope not. I've seen her before in a bedroom on this floor when all this madness started. Scared the life out of me I can tell you.'

Steve reached out and held her hand. 'But you seem to accept all this so easily, I mean, the supernatural, ghosts?'

Tara smiled, something that could warm the most chilled of men's hearts. 'Well, remember who my father was. Hardly surprising, is it?' The tough and courageous Tara took a step towards the front door, unlatched it and opened it just wide enough to place her head through the gap and look around. The apparition was gone. She retreated inside, closed the door, and hooked on the safety chain.

'Tara, about that safety chain. It's nowhere near strong enough. I do worry about your safety.'

Tara grasped Steve's hand and pulled him to his feet. 'Bless you, darling. Always thinking like a policeman. Come back to bed, I think we have some unfinished business that needs investigating.'

## Chapter 40

Rita Rawlson stood at the French windows of her bedroom, which opened out onto the balcony. In her bed was a man thirty-five years her junior. It was the second of a dead, decapitated seagull hitting one of the windows of the French doors that had caused her to rise, reluctantly, from her bed.

The young man lay, his body covered only from the waist down by the bedclothes.

'What was it, Rita?'

Rita's eyes followed the streak of blood on the glass. She swallowed. A little regurgitated acid burned her throat. 'Oh, nothing. Just a seagull that flew into the window.' She turned to face the young man and undid the cord surrounding her dressing gown and let it fall open, revealing her ageing, naked body. She took a few steps towards the bed. 'Now, where were we?'

From behind her came a voice she recognised but wished she hadn't heard. 'I think we were at the point where we had reached an agreement that you were going to recover that chest from Norton, using similar techniques to those you are obviously using on this young man, you disgusting cow! And cover yourself up. I don't want an eyeful of your sagging body.'

The young man rose naked from the bed, and walked towards Masterton, gently pushing Rita to one side. 'Who the fuck are you, old man, and how the fuck did you get in here? It wasn't a

seagull was it, Rita? It was this twisted voyeuristic old bastard!'
Rita stood in silence. 'Listen, old man, I don't really give a fuck
who you are, but you don't come in here insulting Mrs er ...?'
'Rawlson!' Rita spat out her name.

'Yeah, Rawlson, Rita Rawlson,' the young man said, his face
now in Masterton's. 'You apologise to the lady or I'll ...'

Masterton smiled. 'Or you'll what? With that, he withdrew
the knife from beneath his coat and swung it up so that it rested against the young man's chin.

'Or, or ... I'll leave you alone to talk to Rita!'

Masterton lowered the knife and with the tip he closed the
widening gap in the front of Rita's dressing gown. 'Good deci-
sion, young man. Now go and put some clothes on to save the
townsfolk from the sight of your scrawny body, then fuck off!'

The young man wriggled into his trousers, bundled the rest
of his clothes against his chest and ran, barefoot, out of Rita's
bedroom.

'Right then, Rawlson!' Masterton advanced further into the
room. 'You failed miserably at the task I set you, and by rights,
you should be severely punished, but I'm feeling benevolent. I
really don't know why. You're not going to be forgiven though.
You're going to assist me by becoming one of the Brethren, and
when my things are returned to me – as I'm confident they will
be – there will be a ritual held to summon the Master in which
you will perform an important role: the sacrifice of a child.'

Masterton knew his time was fast running out. He walked to
Rita's bed and slumped heavily down upon it. He must perform
the ritual soon. Rita remained silent. Masterton drew a wheezing breath. 'Don't just stand there, woman. Get some clothes on
that disgusting body. You're coming with me. We have an initi-
ation ceremony to organise.'

PC Murray sat in a seaside shelter facing the road. From all around
him, came the thud, thud of decapitated seagulls falling, inter-
laced with the occasional blood-curdling scream or a cry for help.
Behind him, the large black birds continued to circle above the

pier head, the characteristic caw caw sound they made identifying their type. Murray thought he heard his name being called. He turned to look in the direction from which he thought the call had come. Through the half-darkness, he saw a figure some distance away. He called out, 'Hello!' The figure held up a hand.

'PC Murray? It's Craig Norton. Are you alright?'

Norton moved closer, dodging the carcasses of seagulls on the ground and carefully avoiding those still falling.

Murray called out, 'No. Not really. What on earth is happening?'

Moments later, Norton joined him in the relative safety of the shelter. He settled himself on the wooden bench. 'It would take too long to explain, Constable Murray, and I don't think a seaside shelter is the place to be amidst all that's happening. Follow me. I know somewhere close by where we can at least sit it out for a while.'

Together, the pair raised themselves from the bench. Craig Norton had a wry smile upon his face. 'Look out for the seagulls though. I never knew they could be more dangerous dead than alive!'

Norton led the constable slowly to his aunt's fortune-telling kiosk, fumbled in his overcoat pocket for the keys and unlocked the door, then stepped inside, beckoning for Murray to follow. In what little light entered through the open door, Norton raised the glass of the storm lantern that sat upon the small round table that Madame Volatska used for her readings. He took a box of matches from his pocket, struck one, touched it to the wick and lowered the glass. With a little adjustment, the inside of the kiosk was flooded with its comforting orange light. He motioned to Murray to sit on one of the two chairs that were arranged at the table opposite each other. Above them, the thud of decapitated seagulls striking the roof continued.

Craig forced a smile. 'Well, Murray, I can't tell fortunes, but what I can say is that it's not going to be a good night. But if I get my way, these disturbances will soon be over.'

Before Murray could answer, his attention was taken by a knocking noise from just by his chair. Looking down, in the dull orange glow of the lamp, he could see a dark wooden box the chest, rocking back and forth. He looked up at Norton whose face was seemingly changed by the flickering of the light. The shock made the constable pause for a moment. 'What's in there, Norton? An animal or something?'

Norton's face seemed to change again. 'You wouldn't believe me if I told you, Constable Murray!'

Outside, a woman screamed and a man called out, 'Murderer!'

Murray turned to face the door of the kiosk. 'I really should be out there, Mr Norton. People need my help.'

Norton reached out to the lamp and turned the control to raise the diminishing wick a little higher. The light increased, the trunk continued to rock. 'Forget it, Murray. The people you're hearing, they're beyond help.'

Murray turned back to face a now more familiar-faced Craig Norton. 'What do you mean? It's my duty as a constable to do my best for those people.'

'PC Murray, I don't think you quite understand what I said. Those people are beyond help, because they're already dead. You see, what we've been experiencing recently is a replay of all the evil events that have taken place in this town over the past fifty years – since Simon Clark-Mathos placed his curse on the town.'

The thuds of falling seagulls had ceased, and the cawing of the crows with it. Outside, the distant chimes of an ice cream van could be heard. Norton looked at his wrist-watch, stood, turned down the wick of the lamp until it extinguished and said, 'Come with me, Murray. Let me show you something.'

The chest rose and dropped heavily several times and then stopped.


## Chapter 41

Debbie Barry had cried herself into a disturbed sleep. She lay fully dressed upon the bedclothes. She stirred, looked at the clock. Had she really been asleep for over an hour? From the room next door, the nursery, she thought she heard a sound. Rubbing her weary eyes, she lay still, listening. There it was again. It sounded like a cat scratching on a carpet, pulling at the weave. Then came a deep guttural growl, that of a creature, which when combined in her mind with the scratching, summoned visions of a tiger. Fear rose within her. She lay motionless, as if the slightest sound might alert the creature to her presence, but then, the growling and the scratching stopped, to be replaced by the sound of a baby's pitiful crying. Fear fell away as the thought filled her mind that somehow her missing child had, by some miracle, returned.

She raised her body and sat upon the bed, her feet on the floor. The sound of crying filled her ears. Standing, she made her way to the bedroom door, opened it, and stepped out onto the landing beyond. The crying intensified, but she hesitated before the nursery door. The child behind was now drawing rapid breaths between cries as more air was required to continue the relentless sobs. She could bear it no more. Squeezing the door handle, in a single movement the desperate mother pushed it down and burst into the room.

The freezing cold room was illuminated by a blue almost purple glow, so bright that she didn't pause to turn on the light. Beneath the coverlet in the cot, something writhed and sobbed. Her missing child? Standing by the side of the cot, she reached down and pulled away the covering. The crying stopped instantly and was replaced by a gurgling, hissing sound that came from a dark, wriggling something with eyes that glowed a dull red, teeth sharp and yellow. It exhaled a foetid breath and for a moment lay perfectly still looking up at Debbie.

With no warning, a short arm that ended not in a hand but a three-toed foot-like appendage, the tips of which ended in claws, lashed out from the creature's side. Before she could withdraw her arm, a revolting, hooded claw tore down Debbie's skin. She shrieked, the pain for a moment intense, and jumped back from the cot and stood flat against the wall, her blood staining the wallpaper behind her. Raising eyes, that for more than a minute had been trained upon the cot, she looked towards an opposite corner of the room. There stood a figure wrapped in a white sheet, a mortuary sheet. Frank Chapley. Debbie gasped.

Chapley walked up to the cot and bent down so his face was level with that of the creature who lay writhing and hissing. Chapley raised his head, then turned to look at a trembling Debbie. He smiled and for a moment Debbie felt strangely comforted. The dead man looked down upon the creature in the cot:

'Child from hell, return from whence you came. To the fires that have burned for eternity. Take your evil away from this place, you product of a sick and twisted mind. Go back and join the other servants of Clark-Mathos!'

From the cot there was a burst of what looked like flames, a hissing scream and then the creature was gone.

Chapley stood, turned towards Debbie and smiled.

Still trembling, Debbie mouthed the words, 'Thank you.'

But Chapley was gone.


Moira Taggart felt strangely calm. In her now unlit front room, she pulled back the curtains to allow light from the street outside to enter. Carefully, she made her way across the room, the glass of the exploded light bulb crunching beneath her flimsy slippers. She picked up the bag which shook in her hand, almost overpowering her weak grip. Passing the radio that sat almost silent, the station to which it was tuned having closed down for the night, she reached out to turn it off.

As she did, the radio crackled and a girl's voice, now familiar to her, spoke above the noise. 'Thank you.'

Moira rotated the volume control until there was a click and the radio fell silent. She left the room and slowly made the short walk to her bedroom. She didn't know why, but she knew it was important that the bag remain close by during the night.


Nathaniel Masterton, knife held firmly in hand, had frog-marched Rita Rawlson the short distance from her home to the Empire Ballroom, but not before having forced her to swallow two pink pills which he had taken from his pocket. By now, Rita was feeling light-headed and euphoric. The effort of the past hour had left Masterton feeling weak. He struggled to shift the large sheet of plywood that covered the rear entrance to the ballroom, and when he did, he leant heavily against the door frame for support as he wheezed and coughed. With a light push the heavily drugged Rita was inside. 'Come on, Rawlson. Let's turn you over to the dark side!'

In the gloom, he led Rita by the hand along the corridor that led from the rear entrance into the ballroom itself. When they were a few feet inside, he stopped and placed a hand on her shoulder to indicate that she should do the same. Taking a deep, wheezing breath he chanted an incantation:

'Brethren beyond, bring illumination to this place of darkness in order that I may carry on your dark work in light.'

A few seconds later, the entire ballroom was filled with a blue almost purple light. By now, Rita was becoming unsteady.

'Lie down, woman!' Masterton barked. 'But before you do, get rid of the dressing gown. I'm going to need you naked.' Rita, in her woozy, euphoric state, obliged willingly. Masterton turned his head away. 'Woman, you truly are disgusting!'

From his pocket, he took a small bottle, the cap of which he unscrewed. From beneath his coat, he took the knife. He poured the contents of the bottle over the blade and knelt down beside Rita, who struggled to stay conscious. Lowering the knife to her breasts, Masterton drew a flat side of the blade from left to right.

'Brethren, take this woman into your midst. Make her your servant that she will obey your commands and serve my wishes. As tradition holds, I have anointed her with the blood of one sacrificed to our cause. Her husband's death shall be her saving.'

Rita lay still, her eyes wide open. The floor of the ballroom shook, there was a blinding flash of light and then darkness. For a few seconds, a stillness pervaded, and Masterton held his breath. Slowly the blue almost purple light returned, dim at first, almost imperceptible, but steadily growing in brightness.

Masterton squinted, looked around himself and shouted, 'Shit! No!'

Around the edges of the ballroom and slowly advancing towards him were a number of the dead, some victims of the fire in that very building fifty years before, their souls unable to escape their place of death, it coming so suddenly. Dead with a fifty-year-old grudge to settle with the man who stood before them.

Throwing the knife to the floor, Masterton turned and ran towards the door through which he and Rita had entered, tripping and stumbling over the uneven and broken surface of the floor. For a moment, he paused, turned, and looked behind himself. The dead were gone, the strange light began to fade. There was the sound of footsteps behind him and the beam of a torch swept the floor and then the balconies. Masterton turned, and in the dim light he made out the face of Craig Norton. Beside him wielding the torch was PC Murray.

Norton took a step forward. 'Masterton. What an unpleasant although not unexpected surprise!' Murray Shone the torch beam in Masterton's face. Raising a hand he covered his eyes.

'Leave me alone, Norton, and get your friend in blue to get that torch out of my face!'

Murray lowered the beam of the torch to the floor. The shaft of light, scanning left to right, picked up the glint of the knife on which some blood remained, and then illuminated the prone body of Rita Rawlson. Murray held the beam on her naked body. 'And what's been going on here? I think you have some explaining to do.'

Masterton spat at Murray's boots. 'Fuck you, bluebottle! You're better at demolition than you are at policing!' And he laughed. Rita stirred and groaned. 'Out of my way, copper, and you, Craig bloody Norton!'

Masterton turned and looked down upon Rita Rawlson. 'Sister of darkness, rise up and do your work for the Brethren!'

He turned and stood, facing Norton and Murray. 'I'll leave you with our newly enrolled sister. I shan't be attending your funerals, by the way.'

Behind him, the naked Rita Rawlson rose from the floor, pausing to pick up the knife.

Masterton stepped towards Norton until their faces were separated by inches. 'By the way, Norton. Before she kills you, Rita here will be wanting you to tell her where you've hidden my stuff. Goodbye, you irritating, insignificant mortal!'

Masterton walked briskly towards the rear entrance of the building, one arm held high, laughing as he went.

Norton and Murray turned to face Rita, who had by now thrown her dressing gown loosely around herself. She dropped the knife to the floor and rocked unsteadily on her feet.

'Craig, thank goodness! That excuse for a man, Masterton, thinks he's converted me to be one of his. He mentioned child sacrifice, sick bastard! I played along as I reckon he would have killed me otherwise. Goodness only knows what he drugged me with, but a girl who can cope with fifteen vodka and tonics a night is not easily taken down!'

Norton stepped to Rita's side and steadied her. 'Rita, our last meeting might not have been, well, shall we just say, *appropriate*? You were in fear of your life though, I guess? If you can keep up the facade for another twenty-four hours – and I will help you – you will be able to do the town and me a great service. PC Murray here will take you home. You can't be seen with me.'

Norton walked the still unsteady Rita to Murray's side. Murray linked arms with a grateful but now somewhat embarrassed Rita.

'I'm so sorry, constable, you seeing me like that.'

Murray smiled, then addressed Craig. 'Mr Norton, when we left the kiosk, you said you wanted to show me something. What was it?'

'I think, Murray, that you've seen all you will for one night. The real show begins tomorrow.'

Moments later, Norton, Murray, and a shivering Rita Rawlson were standing outside the old Empire Ballroom. It was late, the town had fallen silent. Behind closed doors and curtains, some slept, some lay awake, but many wondered at the strange events of that evening.

# Chapter 42

## Day Five

In the early hours of the next morning, the first to see the feathered corpse-littered streets were the postman, the milkman, and the paperboys, who in darkness had to sidestep the ghastly, blood-soaked remains. Craig Norton had stayed awake much of the night, planning how best to execute his plan. His aunt had risen very early after a fitful night. She sat, wrapped in her dressing gown, at her kitchen table, a freshly lit cigarette in hand, awaiting the delivery of her newspaper.

Steve Bardon was also awake early with a dozing Tara at his side at the Beach View Hotel. His shift was due to start in less than an hour. Wearing only his underwear, he parted the bedroom curtains just enough to allow him to look out onto the street below. Straining his still bleary eyes against the half-darkness, he looked across the promenade. 'Shit!' Tara stirred, pulling the bedclothes up to stay warm.

'What, what the …? What is it, Steve?'

'Dead seagulls. Hundreds of them, *again!*'

Tara rubbed her eyes. 'Really? How the hell?'

Steve Bardon closed the curtains. 'And what was that about last night? That woman? Things are getting weirder by the day around here. I'd better get a move on and get over to the station, get a briefing from Murray before he goes off duty.'

Tara pulled the covers away from the empty side of the bed while simultaneously pulling the half covering her naked body down to waist level. 'But not before I've given you a debriefing, Constable Bardon!'

Moira Taggart was already up and about by five o'clock, but then she usually was. She sat in her dark front room, dark because the shattered light bulb had not been replaced and the broken table lamp no longer worked. The only light came from the two-bar electric fire, which warmed little but her aged, bony feet.

Her thoughts were only of the duty she must perform, and she somehow knew it must be performed that day.

Debbie Barry had sat downstairs since her experience in the night. She had slept fitfully between bouts of desperate crying. Through a gap in the curtains, she was aware it was becoming light outside. She raised her aching body from the sofa. The pain of moving her stiff joints causing an agonising cry. She needed to use the bathroom, although going upstairs was not something that sat well with her. Rotating her tongue around her dry mouth, she made her way to the kitchen, poured herself a glass of water and returned to the living room.

As she passed near to the mirror that hung in the hallway, she stopped, took a step back and looked at her reflection. The semi-darkness did her image no favours. For a moment she stood, glass in hand, staring. Staring not just at her own reflection, but also the reflection of an elderly man, wrapped in a white sheet. Frank Chapley. She no longer feared this man she knew was dead, in fact, quite the opposite. Without turning, her eyes fixed upon his reflection, from a dry throat she croaked, 'Hello.'

Chapley moved closer behind her. A chill movement of air made Debbie shiver. Chapley moved even closer. 'Good morning. I'm sorry if I startled you, but it was important that I saw you were alright after that awful experience last night. I know it's hard to accept the word of a dead man, but you *will* be reunited with your child, and soon.'

Debbie closed her eyes, tiredness now taking over. Under her breath, she whispered, 'Thank you.'

When she opened her eyes again, Chapley was gone.

Mary Sharp filled the kettle, lit a cigarette, her third that morning, and sat down at the kitchen table. From the other side of the hallway, she heard the click of her nephew's bedroom door being unlatched. Exhaling a cloud of blue smoke, she stood and returned to the now boiling kettle.

'I'll have a coffee too please, Mary – when the fog has cleared!'

Mary took two mugs from a shelf. 'Craig, my dear, it's my home and if I want to fill it with smoke I will.'

Craig took a seat at the table. His aunt placed a steaming mug of coffee in front of him. He raised it to his lips and sipped the warming liquid. 'Quite a night, Mary, but it was what I expected.'

Mary drew on what remained of her cigarette, then blew even more smoke into the room, smiling as she did so. Craig held his breath until the worst of the smoke had disappeared and took another sip of his coffee. Mary stubbed out the butt of her cigarette in the always over full ashtray. 'It's not over is it, Craig?'

'No, but it will be very soon. Like I said, I will need your help though. Tonight.'

Mary nodded and took another cigarette from the nearly empty packet.

'Well, if it's going to be a big day, we need a big breakfast. I wonder if Big Tony has opened today? Silly question really, he would never let a little thing like an invasion of the dead stop him!'

Seashells Cafe was indeed open, although Big Tony doubted that the spread of headless seagull carcasses would help attract business. He opened the front door and looked towards the pier. An open back truck was parked fifty yards away. Two council workers stood by it, large sacks in hand, picking up the dead seagulls with gloved hands and dropping them inside. Tony had carried out some unpleasant tasks in his life, but even so, he wouldn't want to be them.

From the opposite direction, PC Murray, now in civilian clothing, approached. 'You open mate?'

Big Tony turned away from the men engaged in their grim task. 'I don't know what they're going to do with all those. Burn them, I guess? I wouldn't want to be downwind of that bonfire though. Yeah, I'm open. Come in.' Big Tony showed the exhausted young constable to a table in front of the counter where it would be easy to talk to him as he prepared his food. 'What do you fancy? Full English with all the trimmings?' Murray smiled and nodded as he settled into a chair.

'I was out on patrol when those seagulls were raining down. It was horrible. The whole night was very strange. According to that guy Craig Norton, fifty years' worth of bad stuff is being replayed. You know Craig, don't you?'

Big Tony nodded as he turned sausages in a pan. 'Yeah. Sure, I know him. Madame Volatska's nephew. I reckon that if she actually could tell fortunes, she would have known all this shit was going to happen.' He pushed a mug of tea across the counter.

'Well, Norton knows a lot about it, or he says he does.'

The bell above the front door rang as Craig Norton pushed it open, standing aside as he ushered his aunt inside. Big Tony began to arrange Murray's breakfast on a plate. 'Well, there's the man himself. Let's ask him.'

Masterton was sitting on a bench opposite the closed amusement arcade, looking out to sea. He nodded at the council workmen as they parked and alighted from their truck, pulling fresh sacks from behind the cab. He was finding it hard to breathe. His whole body ached. If he didn't find the chest and perform the ceremony to raise his master and plead for an extension to his life as a servant of the Brethren of the Visiting Spirits, he knew he would soon be finished. The way he felt that morning, he was sure the time was soon coming. He barely had the strength to raise himself from the bench to go and find Norton, let alone challenge him again about the whereabouts of the chest.

The doors of the council truck slammed shut and it rumbled slowly away to the west, leaving behind it a cloud of diesel smoke that made Masterton cough uncontrollably.

Rita Rawlson had slept in. When she awoke, she felt drowsy and sick and had barely any recollection of what had happened the previous night. She turned over and looked at the floor beside the bed. The sight of her filthy dressing gown triggered memories. Masterton, the pills, the old Empire Ballroom, Craig Norton, and the constable. They would have seen her naked. She felt somewhat excited by the thought. Raising herself from the bed, she sat for a moment on the edge while she waited for a feeling of nausea to clear. Then she stood, walked over to the full-length mirror on the wardrobe door and looked at the reflection of her naked body. *Not bad for my age*, she thought. Then she smiled and thought that maybe, soon, she might make a play for one of the town's handsome young constables.

Talk at Seashells Cafe had become animated as Norton, Murray, Mary Sharp and Big Tony discussed the events of the previous night. Murray placed his knife and fork on his empty plate, downed the dregs of his tea, and chose a lull in the conversation to say something that made Craig Norton's heart sink.

'What was going on with that chest in the fortune-telling kiosk? You've got some animal in there for sure. That can't be right.'

Mary Sharp stared at her nephew. It was clear she was just as concerned as he was. Big Tony wiped his hands on his apron and frowned. 'What chest is that then, eh, Norton? Sounds interesting.'

Norton swallowed. 'Oh, it's nothing. Just some of my stuff.'

Over the noise of the conversation, none of them had heard the bell above the door ring again. From a nearby table, an angry voice called out. 'I think you mean *my* stuff, Norton! So that's where you're hiding it.'

There was silence as everyone turned to face Masterton, who sat glaring angrily at the speechless Craig Norton.

# Chapter 43

PC Bardon, sporting an immaculate uniform, lovingly washed and ironed by the voluptuous landlady, Tara Jones, made his way on foot from the police station to the seafront, pausing momentarily to take in the sight of the dead and decapitated seagulls. Stopping to look through the window of Woolworths, he was aware in the reflection that a heavily made-up Rita Rawlson had come up behind him.

'Good morning, handsome, I mean, officer!' Bardon jumped to one side and turned, his nose twitching from the smell of over applied perfume. 'I suppose you heard what happened to me last night? I still don't feel right, you know.' Rita took a perfectly folded, monogrammed handkerchief from her handbag and dabbed the corner of her eyes.

PC Bardon raised his left arm, linking it with Rita's right. 'Yes, Constable Murray told me. I'm very sorry. Come on, let's walk together and you can fill me in on the finer points.' Rita tried to look wronged and upset but could barely suppress a smile.

'It was horrible. That awful man Masterton drugged me, and, this is so embarrassing, made me strip naked in the old Empire Ballroom.'

The unlikely pair continued to walk arm in arm towards the promenade, Rita barely pausing for breath. At the bottom of one of the three roads that linked the High Street to the seafront, Bardon stopped.

'Well, Rita, it was lovely chatting. I'm going to begin my patrol outside the hotel. I assume you'll be going home to rest if you've not recovered from your ordeal?'

Rita felt a rush of excitement and had to stifle what would have been a girlish giggle.

'Oh yes, I am, PC Bardon. But I'm ever so afraid that I'll encounter Masterton. He's got into my house before, you know. He's got his hands on my keys; I must get the locks changed.'

Against his better judgement, Bardon relented, and still arm in arm, the ageing and frustrated Rita and the handsome young constable turned right and headed towards Rita's house.

Masterton raised himself from his seat in Seashells Cafe, but he was weak and had to lean forward onto the table in front of him for support. His eyes fixed upon Craig Norton. 'I'm a dying man, Norton, but I'm not giving up without a fight. Although I would rather it didn't come to that. I would be willing to do a deal with you.'

In that moment, a plan formed in Norton's mind. He turned and winked at his aunt, who knew from that one small gesture what he wanted her to do. Craig smiled then turned back to face Masterton. 'A deal? Alright, let's talk, Masterton.'

The bell above the door rang as Mary Sharp left. A few minutes later, she would be at her kiosk and the chest would be moved to another, safer, temporary location, back in her flat.

Norton sat opposite a wheezing Masterton. Big Tony leant upon his counter and strained his ears to hear. Masterton cleared his throat which led to another bout of violent coughing, which slowly subsided into wheezing breaths.

'So, Norton. What would it take for you to give my stuff back?'

Norton tried to retain a serious expression. 'What do you have in mind? It's going to need to be good.'

Masterton leaned forward to shorten the distance between himself and Norton after becoming aware that Big Tony was obviously listening. 'I know what a young man like you wants. The love of a beautiful girl, and I know you've had your eye on one. Only she's with someone else, that policeman, Bardon. She could be yours, you know. I could do that for you.'

The thought of the gorgeous hotel proprietor, Tara Jones, made Norton smile.

'I can see you're tempted, Norton. Shall we call it a deal? You return my stuff and she's yours. I shall see to it.'

Norton nodded but did not speak. Yes, he was more than a little attracted to Tara Jones, but he was also a man of honour, although Masterton's proposal would buy him some time.

'Shall we say in two hours' time then, outside Madame Volatska's kiosk? Tara will be with me so my part of the deal will be confirmed.'

Masterton held out his right hand, which Norton took in his and shook. He couldn't help but notice the coldness and the fragility of the old bones beneath the surface of the parchment-thin skin. Looking into the old man's eyes, he knew that time was running out for his nemesis, but not fast enough.

Rita Rawlson and Steve Bardon stood on the pavement outside Rita's house, still arm in arm.

'Steve, sorry, I mean, PC Bardon, would you come inside with me? I'm really worried that horrible man will be in there.' At that moment, the way she felt, Rita wouldn't care what man was inside, she would jump on him and vent her sexual frustration.

'Well, Rita, I'm not sure you do need me with you. Go inside, but leave the front door open. I'll wait here. Call out and let me know you're alright, then I'll close the door and leave.'

Rita was already scheming. 'Alright. I'll go in and check all the rooms and let you know if I need you.' Bardon stood watching. He looked at his wrist-watch. He really should have been back on patrol, not waiting for the all-clear from an ageing, neurotic woman. Several minutes passed. He was about to call out to Rita, when her panicked voice came from somewhere within the house.

'PC Bardon! Quick! I'm upstairs in the bedroom.' Bardon pushed the front door wide open and strode upstairs, two steps at a time. 'I'm in here, constable!' Rita called out from behind a closed door, which Bardon opened hurriedly, to be presented with the sight of Rita wearing nothing but a suspender belt and stockings, her hands holding up her ample breasts. 'Come on then, you sexy young copper. Restrain me!'

Bardon turned his head to one side. 'Really, Rita! Let's just put this down to the shock of your experience last night and the aftermath of whatever you were drugged with.'

Without looking at her, he took a few steps forward, lifted her dressing gown from the chair beside the bed and held it out in her direction. The craziness of the situation made him smile. He knew it would make Tara smile too when he told her later.

## Chapter 44

At the Beach View Hotel, Tara Jones floated about in a dressing gown, attending to various domestic duties. Float was the right word. She felt lighter than air and for the last couple of days, she had more often than not worn a broad smile on her lovely, rounded face. She had her man and knew it was love. Returning to her bedroom, she dressed and made her way back out to the reception desk. Surprisingly, there were guests due that morning, probably attracted by the ghoulish reports from the town, which had now attracted the attention of the national newspapers.

Stepping through the door behind the desk, she was confronted by a very ill-looking Masterton. 'What the bloody hell do you want? Two words. Fuck off!' Masterton lowered himself into one of the reception chairs. 'I'm warning you, old man. PC Bardon is out the back.'

Masterton flashed a sickly smile. 'Oh no, he's not. I've not long seen him arm in arm with that awful Rawlson woman.'

Tara scowled. 'Liar. You would say anything to get at me!'

'Believe what you want, young lady. Anyway, I've not come here for a fight. Look at me; do I look like I have the strength?'

Tara fixed her eyes on Masterton, who she thought looked ten years older than when she had last seen him. She felt unable to withdraw her gaze.

'I don't know where your stuff is if that's what you're going to ask me.' Masterson's eyes met hers. Tara shuddered.

'Well, fortunately for you, young lady, I know exactly where it is, and Norton has agreed to hand it back to me, in exchange for a little favour, which is where you come in.'

Tara couldn't take her eyes away from Masterton's stare. She felt strange, light-headed. Masterton's eyes seemed to become larger. 'I'm not getting involved in your schemes, you absolute bastard!' All she was aware of were Masterton's eyes, from which she couldn't look away.

'Tara, you are in love with Craig Norton. You have been since you first saw him. You want him. All you want is to tell him, to be with him. I'm going to turn away from you now, and when you come round, which will happen as soon as I leave, the idea of being with Norton will become an obsession.'

Tara was suddenly aware she had lost a couple of minutes. Masterton was gone. Her mind was filled with thoughts of Craig

Norton. Her heart raced. She felt flushed. Her passion for a man she hardly knew ran high.

Steve Bardon had managed to get out of Rita Rawlson's house without further unwanted advances and was now heading to where he should have started his beat nearly an hour before outside the Beach View Hotel. He couldn't hold back the smile that was gradually spreading across his face.

Rita swore and threw off her dressing gown, lay on her bed, unsatisfied and frustrated. Within ten minutes she was asleep

The town had come to life in a way that wasn't usual for the time of year. Many had been drawn out of their homes to investigate the strange happenings of the previous night. The council workers had been busy collecting the many dead decapitated seagulls, but many still remained where they had fallen from the sky.

A single crow stood upon the seawall, twisting its black head from side to side, seemingly impressed by the sight of the three headless seagulls that lay on the pavement at the foot of the wall. Raising its beak to the sky, it let out the familiar caw caw sound, a sound that many had been disturbed by just a few hours before.

As PC Bardon made his way along the seafront, he was stopped every few yards by people wanting to know what had happened. He presented to them a version of events that he thought would satisfy their needs, but which he was sure hadn't to judge by the incredulous looks upon their faces. Occasionally, his steady policeman's stride was halted as he examined things clearly disturbed by the previous night's activity, things where they shouldn't be. A single man's shoe by a bench, a lady's coat speckled with what looked like blood. A child's teddy bear, which he picked up and placed in one of his large coat pockets, thinking that such a thing of innocence should not be part of all this. In a few minutes' time, he would be outside the Beach View Hotel. He hoped to spend a few minutes with Tara. After all, it was his duty as a policeman to inquire after the well-being of the public he served

Big Tony was taking full advantage of the unexpected swelling of visitors to the town. Seashells Cafe was full, and Tony's arms whirled like those of a conductor in front of an orchestra as they darted between high shelves and pans of sausages, bacon and eggs frying upon the hob.

A man in a long beige overcoat sat at a table in front of the counter, a notebook and pen beside his mug of tea. He called over to Big Tony. 'Excuse me, mate. Great breakfast, by the way. I'm Phil Ryan, journalist with a national newspaper. Think you could give me an angle on what's been going on around here? You probably meet more folk in a day than most.'

The larger-than-life cafe owner plated up the last of the current breakfast orders and shouted out a table number. 'Fifteen!'

'Well, I've overheard a few things that might interest you. I'll come round in a minute. Another tea? On the house.' Big Tony didn't know much, but he was a great storyteller who could embellish the smallest of gossip.

Ten minutes later, the journalist believed he had the makings of a couple of sensational columns.

PC Bardon had reached the Beach View Hotel, the start of his beat, and home to the girl he now knew he loved. He paused before entering the reception area, straightened his tie, and cleared his throat before pushing open the door. He walked up to the reception desk and rang the brass bell. A few seconds passed before a flustered Tara Jones appeared in the doorway behind the desk.

'Good morning, officer. Something I can help you with?' The young constable smiled, assuming that his girlfriend's official manner was part of a joke at his expense.

'Well, yes, my darling. A kiss would be nice!' Tara frowned.

'I don't think I should. What if Craig were to find out?'

Bardon fixed Tara in his gaze. 'Craig? Craig Norton? What the hell has it got to do with him?'

A tear rolled down Tara's right cheek. 'Because I love him, that's what.'

The policeman's heart sank. 'But Tara, when? Why?'

Tears now flooded from Tara's eyes. 'I don't know. I just do. I have to see him, soon.'

Unnoticed by Bardon, Masterton was standing behind him. Only when the old man emitted a wheezing cough did he turn. For a moment the pair stared at each other in silence, before Masterton stepped aside to allow himself a clear view of the tearful Tara. 'Come on, young lady. I need you. I'll take you to your lover. He'll be waiting.'

Bardon stepped up to the reception desk to prevent Tara from exiting. 'Don't go, Tara, please. This is all some horrible trick. He's got you hypnotised or something.'

Masterton was struggling for breath and Tara was beating her fists upon Steve Bardon's chest as he attempted to grab her wrists.

Masterton stood close behind. 'Step aside, copper. Let her go. It's clear that it's not you she wants!'

Bardon, feeling he had no choice, stepped aside, clearing the way for Tara to run to the door by which she left, dressed only in a thin blouse under a cardigan and a short skirt. She was followed closely by a wheezing and coughing Masterton.

## Chapter 45

At the Ship and Anchor, Ken Lomes was also benefiting from the unseasonal upturn in trade. He took a pint glass from the shelf above the bar and held it below a tap as he pulled a wooden handle. 'A pint of Best on its way, Mr Norton. How are your inquiries going? Last night was awful.' Craig took his pint of beer from Ken and placed it upon a beer mat on the bar.

'Indeed, Ken. They're more than just inquiries now. That's the reason I've come to see you. If you have customers asking about what's happening, and they mention the old Empire Ballroom, try and discourage them from going there. After all, they can't get in, unless they're intent on trespass. I need the place to myself later – at least myself and a few others.'

Ken took a glass from the shelf and began to serve another customer. 'I'll do my best, but you know how inquisitive people can be. A pint of Best and a Babycham wasn't it, sir?'

Unnoticed by Norton, Masterton, followed by Tara Jones, passed by the pub windows. He looked at his watch. There was thirty minutes before he was supposed to meet Masterton outside his aunt's kiosk.

Steve Bardon allowed a couple of minutes to pass before he followed Masterton and Tara Jones along the promenade. He felt this was less likely to inflame Masterton's temper, although he kept them in sight as he walked. A sound was brought to him on the westerly breeze, the chimes of an ice cream van that became steadily louder until it loomed into view, swerving erratically at pedestrians who leapt out of its path, some waving fists, some tripping and stumbling to the ground. Within a minute, the van passed him, the driver, who Bardon now knew to be deceased, grinning, his right hand raised in a thumbs-up gesture. Much as he knew it was his duty to deal with this menace to public safety, he was on foot, and the ice cream van was already nearly one hundred yards away behind him. Besides, there was a worse threat: the incoming of evil that was causing chaos in the town and could well result in injuries, or worse.

Placing his empty glass upon the bar, Craig Norton thanked a busy Ken Lomes, who was very glad that his somewhat unreliable new barmaid, Julie, had been able to assist him on what should have been a quiet, late autumn day. Craig now had ten minutes until his appointment with Masterton. He walked slowly, the chill breeze making him shudder. He knew that Masterton 's rage would be immeasurable, and Craig questioned his actions, but after all, Masterton was an old man who had become progressively weaker over the past couple of days, and it was better for Norton to keep tabs on his adversary. He might have been weak, but his magical power, Norton guessed, would still be strong. And to suffer some sort of remote psychic attack at this critical point was something he did not want to consider.

As he drew level with the kiosk on the opposite side of the promenade, the sight of Masterton and Tara Jones made him pause, but any ideas of turning back, as Masterton turned and held him in his gaze, were out of the question.

Tara's heart leapt and, despite the seafront road being used by inquisitive tourists now shipping out of town, she ran, arms outstretched towards Craig Norton, in front of a Triumph Herald that braked heavily, the driver shouting abuse from inside. A few seconds later, running at speed, Bardon was by Tara's side, escorting her gently onto the pavement. The confused hotel proprietor stared at him, her eyes glazed, her mouth open.

'Tara, you could have been killed!' Bardon stood to one side and motioned to the Triumph to move on.

'Yes, thank you, constable. I'll be alright. It was the excitement of seeing my boyfriend. I'll be fine now.'

Norton stood in silence, his eyes fixed on Bardon as Tara threw her arms around him and planted a kiss on his cheek. But despite the strangeness of the situation, having this gorgeous young woman's body pressed tight against him released a sense of power within him.

From the opposite pavement Masterton called out, 'Norton, get over here now! I've upheld my part of the deal. I want my stuff and I'm running out of patience!'

Norton mouthed the word 'sorry' to PC Bardon and nodded. He knew he had less than a minute to come up with a plan. He'd outwitted Masterton before, but this would be direct conflict, and given the old man's weakened state, it was likely he would resort to sorcery to settle the matter.

As the last of the flurry of traffic passed, relative silence returned to the seafront. In the distance, but becoming increasingly louder, the chimes of the ice cream van could be heard, now sounding more out of place than ever to Norton's ears. He stared fixedly at Masterton as he crossed the road.

From behind him he could hear Tara shouting, 'Craig, be careful. I love you!'

A couple of seconds passed and his right foot mounted the kerb on Masterton's side. His eyes were still fixed on the old man, but something was happening, he assumed, to his vision. Masterton's image was beginning to fade in and out like some cheap special effect in a science fiction film. Then, after a few seconds, all that was visible was a fading outline.

Masterton's voice, somehow distant called out, 'It's nearly over for me, you bastard, Norton. This isn't over between *us* yet though!'

Norton stood, staring at nothing, just an empty space where his adversary had been just moments before. His stomach leapt upwards as right behind him the ice cream van began its chiming once again. The sky began to darken, and an electrical charge seemed almost to crackle in the air. In the distance, thunder rumbled, and the first heavy raindrops began to pelt against the pavement in front of Norton. He stood still, allowing his clothes to become soaked through. He knew something was very wrong, but what? And where was Masterton? Had Norton got away with his confrontation and his lie to him regarding the whereabouts of the trunk?

## Chapter 46

Mary Sharp jumped up from her seat at the kitchen table at the sound of rain in order to close the window that she had opened earlier to let out the cigarette smoke from the kitchen that even she now felt uncomfortable with sitting in.

Seashells Cafe was empty, and with the weather now set wet for the rest of the day, Big Tony locked the front door and turned the cardboard sign to closed. He'd made enough money that morning to allow himself a quiet late afternoon and evening, and if the rain relented later, He would take a well-earned stroll in the evening air.

Moira Taggart had heard the rain against her front room window from where she had been sitting in front of her two-bar electric fire listening to the radio. Remembering she had washing hanging out on the line, she raised herself stiffly from the chair in which she was sitting and took a few slow and careful steps to the door.

The voice of the presenter on the radio faded, followed by a crackle, then a girl's voice said, 'It has to be today. Thank you!'

Debbie Barry stood in her son's nursery, staring at his empty cot as raindrops pattered heavily against the window. She felt strangely calm, and a feeling of hope had returned. Was it because outside, Frank Chapley stood, wrapped in his white mortuary sheet, staring up at the window of the nursery?

With the day becoming increasingly dark, Ken Lomes had turned on the lights in the now almost empty saloon bar of the Ship and Anchor. His barmaid, Julie, sat at a table filing her nails and applying polish.

'Ken, I don't like it.'

'Don't like what, Julie? The colour of your nail polish?'

'No, Ken. Although I'm not that keen now I've seen it on. I mean, the day, this sudden turn in the weather. It's ominous. I have a bad feeling, a feeling that something is going to happen.'

Ken smiled, but he felt suddenly sad. It was at times like this that he missed Dennis. They would have had the cards out and a bottle of whisky on the table.

A flash of lightning, followed only a few seconds later by a window-shaking clap of thunder had awoken a still sexually frustrated Rita Rawlson. With one eye open, she turned on her side, took the three-quarter-full bottle of Vodka from her bedside table, raised her head slightly, put the neck of the bottle to her lips and gulped down a mouthful of the neat spirit. It burned her throat. She wanted to forget the last few hours, the last few days.

Craig Norton turned and looked along the promenade at the old Empire Ballroom. A fork of lightning split the sky and the thunder that followed seemed to shake the ground around him. When the sky darkened again, a blue almost purple glow was left above the ballroom. He was now sure what was wrong.

Tonight, the full fury of fifty years of evil would release itself upon the town, resulting in injuries and almost certainly deaths, unless he enacted his plan. He knew that he hadn't seen the last of Masterton. Somewhere, somehow, he would be finding a way to re-energise his rapidly ageing body, even if only temporarily. He needed to get back to his aunt's flat and gather all he would need for his plan.

On the roof of the old Empire Ballroom, within the strange blue almost purple glow was the misty outline of a man, an old man who now had virtually no energy, an old man who would soon be just a memory as his mortal body would become nothing more than a weak human with no magical powers, and death would loom large. Within minutes he would decay to the state of the corpse of a man who should have died many years before.

In the distance, thunder rumbled. Then, directly above the ballroom, the storm clouds released a bolt of lightning that illuminated for just a moment, the entire town. It struck the lightning conductor atop the lead-roofed dome that sat above the ballroom's auditorium, in front of which was Masterton's faded outline. From the wide green copper strip that would carry the energy of the lightning away to ground came a spider of electrical throngs that entered Masterton's barely visible body. The sky darkened, the electrical discharge disappeared with a crackle, and Masterton stood, his figure now clear, his energy restored. but he knew this couldn't last. Maybe for a few hours he would be able to function. Hopefully this would be long enough to summon his master and request an extension to his life, but to do that, he would need the contents of the chest, the chest that

Craig Norton was carefully unpacking, checking, and repacking at his aunt's flat in readiness for executing his plan.

Steve Bardon had accompanied a distressed and tearful Tara Jones back to the Beach View Hotel. Her emotional state Bardon put down to whatever magic Masterton had worked upon her. Tara was tired and chilled by the downpour. All she wanted was to sleep. He would see her safely to her bed and return to his beat, a beat that would be the strangest of his career to date.

In the thirty minutes that the constable had been away, the town had become busy, but not busy with the living. The town's residents, most of whom, sensing that something was wrong, remained within their homes and businesses with the lights on against the rapidly unnaturally darkening day. Along the promenade, groups of men and women dressed in styles popular fifty years before wandered towards the old Empire Ballroom. In side streets and alleys, acts of the most atrocious nature were being re-enacted by figures now lost to the grave. All the young constable could do was roam within a town that now seemed consigned to the strangest of fates.

Above all the weirdness and confusion, on the roof of the old Empire Ballroom, Masterton stood, arms outstretched surveying the scene below. He felt invigorated, alive, and he hoped that tonight he would be given the gift of many more years of life. But first, he needed to get back the items that could make it happen.

Moira Taggart worked her arthritic joints into her overcoat, switched off the radio and bent painfully down to pick up the bag she had placed in the hallway after the disembodied voice had spoken through the radio. The bag shook and shuddered. She struggled to hang on to it, but she was acutely aware that she must deliver it to the one person who knew what needed to be done.

As she walked away from her bungalow, she greeted strange figures who walked the pavements. Her eyesight was poor and so she didn't notice the strangeness of these folk with their distorted faces and anachronistic clothing. The bag continued to shake, its contents rattling. Her destination wasn't far away, a small flat owned by Madame Volatska, aka Mary Sharp. A flat where she had heard through gossip, that Mary's nephew, Craig Norton, was staying, a young man who had the power to save the town from the increasing evil that pervaded.

Rita Rawlson lay upon her bed, blankets around her waist, the almost empty bottle of vodka still clutched in her right hand. She had started to drift into an alcohol-induced coma when she heard her name being called from within the room. She raised her heavy sleepy eyelids, which rapidly became wide open. The empty vodka bottle clattered to the floor.

By the curtained French doors stood her dead husband, Dennis. For a moment Rita wasn't sure it was him. How could it be? His image swam up and down in her eyes that were victims of the alcohol. She sat up, and a wave of nausea swept over her. She swallowed the bile that clogged her throat and croaked her husband's name.

'Dennis?' She paused. 'Is it really you?'

'Yes, it's me, Rita.' Her dead husband now stood a few feet away from the bed. Realising she was naked, Rita pulled the bedclothes up in an attempt at modesty. The belated Dennis Rawlson smiled. 'Same old Rita. You seem to forget I've seen it all before, many times.' Rita let the covers drop, exposing her over ample breasts again. Her head swam and she swallowed back more stinging bile. 'Listen to me, Rita. You have to help. You're needed by the people of the town. You're a good woman, Rita, deep down.'

Rita closed her eyes for a moment, her swimming vision was making her nauseous. When she opened them, the image of her husband was gone. She now could not be sure whether her experience had been part of some vodka-induced dream. But whether it had been or not, the message that she had to help remained clearly in her mind.

# Chapter 47

Mary Sharp stood before the bathroom mirror, cigarette in hand. The door of the tiny room was wide open. 'Craig, darling, I thought I heard a knock at the front door. Do you mind going to see who it is?'

Her nephew carefully closed the lid of the trunk, raised himself from the bed upon which he had been sitting and made his way to the front door of the flat. Through the frosted glass he could see that a short figure stood on the other side. He turned the handle and cautiously opened the door, just enough to assess the unexpected visitor. Seeing an old lady, he opened the door wide.

'Mr Norton? I have something for you.' Moira Taggart passed over the bag which she had struggled to carry for twenty minutes, a bag that still shook and rattled as she passed it into Craig Norton's hand. He looked at Moira, confused. 'I was told you would need this.'

Norton held tight to the now violently shaking bag. In the time it took him to ask, 'Won't you come in?' Moira Taggart had turned, raised a hand and was already upon the pavement. Craig called out, 'Thank you – I think!' Then he closed the front door and carried the seemingly possessed cloth bag through to his bedroom where it became impossible to hold. It was leaping out of his hand and seemed almost magnetically attracted to the trunk that stood upon the floor. And then it became motionless. Craig had no clue what was within the bag and he feared opening it for what might be released. Although he felt it contained something of importance, something somehow related to what the trunk contained, the trunk that was now repacked, and which, in a few hours, would play the major role in his plan.

In the streets of the town, the atmosphere was becoming worse, the sky darker. PC Bardon walked his usual beat, warning any townsfolk foolish enough to be outside to go back to their homes and to take the precaution of locking their doors. In the distance, he heard the sound of an ice cream van's chimes.

At the Ship and Anchor, barmaid Julie sat at a table by the window looking out onto the promenade. 'Ken, you know that bad feeling? Well, it's just got worse. I think we should lock the doors.'

Ken Lomes came out from behind the bar and sauntered in the direction of his ditsy barmaid. He looked through the window, took a pace back, and in a voice that was almost a whisper said, 'Yes, Julie. I believe you're right.'

As he turned to make his way to the front door, the phone behind the bar rang, distracting him from his task. Picking up the telephone receiver, he heard a familiar voice. 'Ken, Ken. It's Rita Rawlson. Have you seen Dennis?'

'Rita, have you been drinking? You know as well as I do that Dennis is dead. How could I have seen him?'

'Yes, that's what I thought, Ken, but I saw him in my bedroom earlier. He told me the town needed my help.'

'Rita, I'm not really sure you're completely with it. Go and have a lie down. Maybe another man will appear in your bedroom – if you're lucky.'

'You've got a bloody cheek, Lomes. You never did take me seriously!'

There was a click as Rita angrily replaced the receiver at her end. Ken shook his head and as he turned back to where he had been standing moments before, he called out, 'Julie, that was bloody Rita Rawlson, asking if I'd seen her dead husband of all things!'

There was no reply. He looked across the bar from left to right. Julie had gone and a disgusting smell of seared flesh filled the air.

## Chapter 48

The strange glow above the old Empire Ballroom was becoming brighter. Lightning struck all around, thunder rumbled, but there was no rain now. Masterton stood upon the roof, surveying the town below him. He smiled broadly and began to laugh at the realisation that he no longer needed a plan to recover the chest that contained all he needed to summon his Master. Norton was going to bring it to him, as he was convinced that the activity surrounding the ballroom would attract the pathetic mortal. He could, with his renewed strength, finally tackle the problem. After all, they had shaken hands upon a deal, and he, Masterton had honoured his part. Norton would be a fool to cross him again, although he strongly suspected that he may have his own plan: to raise Simon Clark-Mathos and beg for the town to be released from the curse that tonight, in its final hours, would release a torrent of evil from which this small seaside community may never recover. He would make the young man truly regret his actions up until now. It had to be tonight. The time was right, the build-up of energy was approaching its peak with the power of fifty years of evil and wrongdoing. Lightning struck again at the conductor atop the dome above the theatre, the flash outlining the figure of a man who now believed his future was secure.

PC Bardon looked towards the source of the flash and at Masterton who stood with outstretched arms. He thought of Tara and the spell that had been placed upon her by the old man. Probably a spell that only that evil man could reverse.

Craig Norton picked up the bag that Moira Taggart had brought him. He struggled to pull it away from the chest, and when he had, it shook and the contents rattled. A strong force pulled it back towards the chest again. With some effort, he pulled it away and looped and knotted the top of the bag around the cast iron bed frame. Stooping down, he lifted the chest from the floor and carried it out to the kitchen, the bag rattling and shaking as he exited the bedroom. His Aunt Mary sat at the kitchen table, lit a cigarette, and inhaled deeply. Craig placed the chest upon the table, tipping the contents of the always overfull ashtray in front of his aunt.

'Bloody hell, Craig! Be careful!' Mary Sharp blew out a cloud of blue smoke. 'Who was at the door earlier?'

'Oh, no one important, just someone collecting for charity.'

Mary held the ashtray below the rim of the table and with her right hand swept the cigarette butts, ash and spent matches back into it, blowing away whatever remained. 'So, what's this about? Taking that bloody chest somewhere, are you?'

Craig pulled a chair from beneath the table and sat down beside his aunt, who added yet another smoking cigarette butt to the now slightly emptier ashtray. The thin plume of smoke wavered, then blew towards him making his eyes sting.

'Really, Mary. You should give that up.'

Mary took another cigarette from the half-empty packet upon the table. 'It's one of my only pleasures. And talking of pleasure, when are you going to ask the gorgeous Tara Jones out?'

Craig smiled, dismissing the question. 'Mary, I'm going to need your help. We need to get this stuff over to the old Empire Ballroom. I hate to be dramatic, but time is running out. If I don't carry out my plan today, I don't like to think about the consequences for the town. I will need good people with me. I need their energy to fight against the evil that is building by the hour.'

The telephone rang in the hallway and Craig raised himself from the chair and went to answer it. 'Hello. Mary Sharp's residence.'

For a moment the line was silent, but then came the sound of a girl sobbing, then in between sobs, 'Craig, Craig. It's Tara Jones. I'm sorry. It's just, well, it's just that I want to see you.'

Norton paused before answering, 'Tara, can you get over to my aunt's flat? There's something I want to talk to you about. Something very important. Be really careful though. It's awful outside tonight.'

Tara's sobbing had now calmed. 'Yes, Craig, of course. Anything for you.'

# Chapter 49

PC Bardon continued to walk the streets of the town. All around him, acts of evil were being carried out, but these were acts committed back in time, some before he was even born. Along the promenade, the figures of men and women dressed in a style popular fifty years before were walking in groups towards the old Empire Ballroom.

But within one of the groups was a figure that looked out of place, a young woman dressed in clothing of the day, a young woman Steve recognised. He called out, 'Julie! Are you alright?'

The young barmaid called back, 'No. Not at all. They're taking me somewhere. Help me!'

The group pulled in tight around her until she was no longer visible. All Bardon could do was follow in the wake of the group and see where they were taking her.

He called out, 'Julie. I'm here. I'm following.'

Tara Jones pulled shut and locked the front door of the Beach View Hotel. The guests who had checked in earlier that day had declared the town too weird for comfort and checked out. Beneath her long coat, she wore the lowest of low-cut tops and the shortest of short skirts. She paused momentarily to look at the figures who were heading west along the opposite pavement, but when one turned to look directly at her, she quickly walked on and turned right up the side street beside the hotel. A gust of wind blew open the lower half of her coat, revealing her shapely legs. She grinned as she thought about the treat she would give Craig Norton.

Groups of the dead, with their distorted faces and foul stench of seared flesh, were gathering at the front of the old Empire Ballroom. Masterton looked down upon them and laughed, a laugh that was carried away upon the ever-increasing breeze. He knew that Norton would arrive soon. It was late afternoon, but already the sky had taken on a blue inky darkness, more so than would be normal for the time of year. The darkness was his ally. In darkness, dark acts could be played out unseen, things that stalked the night could once again roam. He turned to look behind himself at the great dome, the blue almost purple glow dancing around it like luminous children around a maypole.

He drew a deep breath and called out, 'Master, tonight, you shall return to be among your people once again.'

The stiff breeze carried his words away. From far below came a muffled scream and a cry for help.

Tara Jones tidied her hair and smiled her sweetest smile, then knocked upon the front door of Mary Sharp's flat. Through a cloud of cigarette smoke Mary winked at her nephew.

'You know who that'll be, Craig. Best go and let the gorgeous thing in.'

Craig shook his head. 'Don't you say anything out of place or make any suggestions, Mary!'

He opened the door slightly and looked through the gap, just to be sure it was who he thought. The sight of a smiling Tara made his heart leap. He opened the door and beckoned her inside. For a moment, all he could do was stare.

Tara giggled. 'Well, aren't you going to take my coat then?' She was already shedding the garment to reveal the top and skirt she had chosen especially for the occasion.

'Yes, of course. Sorry, Tara, and thank you for coming here. I know things aren't good out there.' He took Tara's coat and hung it on one of the hooks beside the front door.

'That's alright, Craig. What's going on out there is nothing to what I've experienced lately. Anyway, doesn't a girl get a welcome kiss?'

Craig moved to kiss her on the cheek, but Tara gently grasped his head and placed her lips firmly against his.

Mary watched candidly from the kitchen doorway and smiled. For fifteen seconds the kiss continued until both Tara and Craig needed air. 'So, Craig, what's this all about, you gorgeous man!'

Craig led her through to the kitchen and directed her to one of the chairs that were arranged around the table. Mary busied herself filling the kettle and taking mugs from the cupboard. 'Well, tonight I believe is a critical time for the town. The evil that has been gathering over the past couple of days will almost certainly reach a peak tonight, and the consequences of that I do not wish to consider, but it would undoubtedly be devastating for the town and its people.' Mary brought a tray to the table.

'Tea or coffee, Tara?' Tara smiled.

'Oh, coffee please, Madame Volatska.'

'So, Tara, as I was saying,' Craig continued, 'I have a plan to finally put an end to what is happening. I need to summon the man the Brethren of the Visiting Spirits called "the Master", your father, and plead with him to release the town from the curse.'

Tara stared intently at him as if hanging on every word. 'But how will you do that? And where?'

'That's where you come into my plan, Tara. Most of what I need is contained in that wooden chest I took from your place. And the instructions for the summoning are contained in the book Mathos wrote. There is however one vital element required that I cannot possibly provide: the sacrifice of a baby.'

Tara's eyes opened wide and for a moment she sat deep in thought. 'And Masterton wants to do the same, right? Hence his desperation to get hold of the chest and why in all probability he knows where that missing baby is.'

Craig sipped his coffee. Mary lit yet another cigarette. 'Clever girl. We know that Masterton is weakening, we know he has lived a lifespan many years more than would be natural, and I don't doubt that it was his master who granted him that extended life. And now he's dying he needs to ask for his life yet again to be extended.'

'But Craig, if what you say is true, he has the advantage. He might not yet have possession of the chest, but he does have the baby and I'm guessing he would be willing to kill you to make his plan complete too.'

Craig reached out and put his right hand on top of Tara's left, a serious expression upon his face. 'Well, I think that having you, the Master's daughter present, would be a powerful attraction. That's if you're willing to be there, of course?'

Tara liked the feel of Craig's warm hand against hers. She knew that she could trust this man, and for the time being at least, she felt she loved. 'Yes, of course. I owe it to the town to help; it's my home and livelihood. But you still haven't told me where this is going to happen?'

Craig smiled warmly. 'Where it all started fifty years ago ... at the old Empire Ballroom.'

Tara leaned forward, beckoned Craig towards her and kissed him.

## Chapter 50

The gathering of the dead outside the old Empire Ballroom had grown in number. They were becoming increasingly restless. Masterton backed away from the edge of the roof and stood behind the dome, out of sight. He knew that the crowd below, many of them killed and disfigured by the events of fifty years before, probably considered him responsible. Just a few days before, this situation wouldn't have caused him the slightest anguish, as then he knew he had the power to defend himself. But not now. His temporary energy boost from the lightning strike was just that, temporary. This energy would be gone in minutes if he took on the angry crowd below, then he would be destroyed. He needed to preserve his strength to take on Craig Norton, to recover the chest that contained all he needed to summon his master, the chest that he could not obtain earlier when his energy was so depleted. He desperately needed his master to grant an extension to his life to allow him to continue the work of the Brethren of the Visiting Spirits, to make the organisation, to which he had been faithful for so many years, great again. All he needed was in that chest, except for the baby. But some forty feet below him, in a tatty cardboard box, covered only with a filthy cloth, a starving baby cried. But it was soon comforted by a man wrapped in a mortuary sheet. Frank Chapley.

Ken Lomes had closed and locked the doors of the Ship and Anchor. Outside, the promenade was all but deserted, the group of the dead having now gathered at the front doors of the old Empire Ballroom. But out of sight, in the streets and down dark alleyways, evil acts were being replayed, unseen. His ditsy but lovable barmaid, Julie, had vanished from the bar, and Ken was sure who had taken her, and in which direction they were headed. He looked up at the dark sky. The past few days had been difficult, not only for him, but for the entire town. A sudden breeze chilled him and he pulled his overcoat tight. Remembering the hip flask containing his favourite whisky that resided in his pocket, he took it out, unscrewed the cap, raised it to his lips, and as he passed the entrance to the pier, he took a long draw of the warming liquid. For a moment, he stood still, allowing the whisky to settle in his stomach.

He heard a familiar voice call out his name, but he knew it could not be. But then it came again.

'Ken. Over here!'

Turning to look in the direction from which the voice had come, the pier entrance, there stood his best friend, his late friend, Dennis Rawlson. Ken squinted, still unsure that he was looking at a man for whose funeral, earlier that day, he had been preparing in his head a speech. He slipped the hip flask back into his pocket. 'Dennis?'

'Yes, Ken, it's me. Listen, Rita needs your help. Her life is crumbling, and she has a duty to perform – a duty to me, a duty to the town – to help defeat the evil that has descended upon this place, evil brought by an organisation that my father attempted to eject from the town.'

As Ken stared, the image of his old friend began to fade. Once more, taking the hip flask from his pocket, Ken called out,

'Of course, Dennis. I miss you!' He emptied the contents of the flask into his mouth and wiped a tear from his right eye with the back of his left hand.

Rita Rawlson was torn between making herself a strong black coffee or opening yet another bottle of vodka. Having filled the kettle, she reached into a cupboard below the sink and took out a full bottle of her preferred tipple.

From behind her came the voice of her dead husband:

'Rita, no! You have work to do. Ken will help you. Go to the old Empire Ballroom.'

Rita put the bottle back in the cupboard and turned, but her dead husband wasn't there.

Craig Norton stood with Tara Jones in the bedroom he currently occupied in his Aunt Mary's flat. Tara found it difficult not to push the man she thought she loved onto the bed and take what she wanted. Her emotions were in turmoil because she was in love with this man, but at the back of her mind she knew she was also in love with another, a man in uniform. But overarching this, it now seemed likely that she would, later, face a father she had never known.

A rattling sound came from one end of the bed. 'Craig! What on earth is in that bag? It's moving!'

Craig Norton breathed in the heady smell of Tara's perfume. Having this gorgeous girl to himself in a bedroom was a powerful aphrodisiac. 'To be honest, Tara, I really don't know. It was given to me by an old lady, and I was told I would need it. And as it seems to be almost magnetically attracted to that chest, I assume it has some relevance to what I have planned for later. Talking of which, we need to make our way to the old Empire Ballroom.' Craig looked out at the rapidly darkening sky beyond the bedroom window. 'And soon, I think.'

# Chapter 51

From behind the dome upon the roof of the old Empire Ballroom, Masterton looked down on the town that spread out in front of him. This was, he guessed, the direction from which Craig Norton would approach, and he was sure that he would have with him what he, Masterton, needed: the chest. Norton knew the consequences of crossing him again. In a few short hours, his life would be extended, maybe by another hundred years or more, and he wouldn't let his master down. The Brethren of the Visiting Spirits would be great and powerful once again and this town would be known as the home of that organisation. And the people of the town, those that did not leave, would be indoctrinated, and become followers. He smiled, then laughed, and that laugh became louder and more maniacal.

Another bolt of lightning struck the lightning conductor above the dome, sending jagged blue forks from anywhere the copper-conducting strips joints had begun to break down. The current below and behind him grew more agitated.

Inside, Frank Chapley hushed the desperately hungry baby in the cardboard box, and placed the by now filthy mortuary sheet over it. Now naked, he slunk off towards the rear of the ballroom, to where his mortal body had been found by those two inquisitive schoolboys.

A low rumble of thunder shook the floors and balconies. Dust cascaded down. The ballroom's long dead caretaker made his way to the foyer, passing over missing sections of the once impressive dance floor as if the missing timber were still present. He swung the doors that allowed access to the ballroom from the foyer wide open, and for a moment it was illuminated by a flash of lightning. Against the grime-encrusted glass entrance doors many heat-distorted faces were pressed, looking into the gloom of the foyer. Systematically, the long-deceased caretaker unlocked the entrance doors and one by one opened them wide, allowing all outside to enter. In orderly lines they proceeded into the ballroom beyond, which was now lit by a dull blue almost purple glow.

Masterton had stepped cautiously towards the parapet of the front wall and looked below. The threat from that crowd had, at least for now, passed.

Craig Norton, assisted by the gorgeous Tara Jones, had taken the chest and the bag, although it had swung resolutely towards the chest, into the kitchen and placed them on the table. His aunt, cigarette in hand stood at the window, seemingly transfixed by the darkness beyond. Her nephew stood behind and to one side of her.

'It looks somehow, I don't know, ominous out there.'

Craig placed his left hand upon her right shoulder and squeezed gently. 'Ominous would be a good way to describe it, Mary, but believe me, if I don't carry out my plan today, it could look a whole lot worse by tomorrow. And some of us may not have a tomorrow if we don't act soon.'

He dropped his hand from his aunt's shoulder and turned to face Tara. 'You will stand by me on this won't you, Tara? I know it's going to be particularly difficult for you. It's possible that you may see your father, or the entity that he now is, destroyed.'

Tara's head dropped slightly, but she kept her eyes upon Craig and forced a weak smile. 'Of course I will. You're a very brave man, Craig Norton.'

Tara's desire for him was the result of a spell, Norton knew that, but those words meant a great deal, and he wished deep down that her love was real. He walked towards the table and placed a hand upon the chest that was central to all he had planned. The bag next to it shook and rattled.

'Mary, Tara, we need to get this stuff down to the old Empire Ballroom and time is of the essence. Mary, if we take a handle of the chest each, Tara, can you carry the bag?'

Tara picked up the writhing and wriggling canvas bag. 'If it keeps struggling like this, it won't be easy!'

Less than a minute later, the trio were outside and walking purposefully in the direction of the promenade.

# Chapter 52

Rita Rawlson looked at herself in the full-length mirror of her bedroom wardrobe and wondered what she had become since her husband's death, from throwing herself at men to nearly becoming the evil plaything of a dangerous power-obsessed old man. The mirror told it all. She looked tired, years older than she had before all this weirdness had begun, but she realised that her husband's words were true. She *could* do some good, help release the town from the grip of evil in which it had been held for four days.

She tidied herself, put on a sober non-revealing black dress, applied the minimum of make-up, and pinned her hair back. Again, she looked at herself in the full-length mirror. The thought crossed her mind that she looked as if she were preparing to attend another funeral as well as that of her late husband, but then it struck her that maybe she would be. But exactly whose she didn't like to guess. She didn't know what she needed to do, but she was pretty sure *where* she needed to do it. In her hallway, she threw on her overcoat, opened the front door, and turned in the direction of the old Empire Ballroom.

Big Tony had taken a late afternoon nap. He had awoken in the semi-darkness and assumed that it was much later than it was. He raised himself lazily from the couch in his small flat and walked to the window with the intention of drawing the curtains against the encroaching darkness, but seeing the long procession of strange figures walking past on the other side of the promenade, and being naturally inquisitive – some might say nosey – he took his coat with which he had covered himself for his nap and hastily made his way outside, locking the front door of his flat behind him.

Keeping pace with the procession of the dead, but on the opposite pavement, he stayed with them until the line broke down into a disorderly group outside the old Empire Ballroom. He kept his distance, partly hidden behind a bus shelter. He heard a girl cry out, 'Help me, somebody please help me!' Through a momentary parting of the figures, he caught a glimpse of a girl he thought he recognised. Doing nothing didn't seem like an option, not when his ego told him he could be a hero and rescue a fair maiden in distress. Stepping out from behind the bus shelter, now charged with bravado, he called out, 'Julie? Is that you?'

Several of the crowd had turned to look at him, while others closed in around the frightened barmaid. Walking towards the crowd, the odour of seared flesh made Tony cough. He cleared his throat and called out again, 'Julie?'

From within the huddle a weak voice called out, 'Tony. Help me!'

A moment later he was in the thick of the strange crowd, who were now forming into an orderly queue. The unlocking of the ballroom doors distracted them, and as they moved slowly forward, Tony was able to reach out and grab Julie's arm. He pulled her, stumbling, to his side. The crowd murmured, some had turned to look at him, but they all now seemed more intent on getting inside the ballroom. Tony let go of Julie's hand. 'You alright, young lady?'

'Yes, thank you so much. A couple of them came into the pub. I'd only just told Ken to lock the doors. They took me with them. I didn't know what they were going to do to me, but I don't suppose it was going to be good?'

Tony grinned and put an arm around Julie's shoulder. 'No problem, lovely. Anything for a pretty girl. The shit keeps getting weirder around here, don't you reckon? I'm going to hang around for a while.'

Julie thanked Tony again, lifted his arm from around her shoulders and headed back along the promenade and up a side street towards her home to change out of clothes now tainted by the smell of burnt flesh.

From the roof at the rear of the old Empire Ballroom, a few hundred yards away, Masterton saw three figures steadily approaching. Two of them separated, apparently carrying something between them, and he had little doubt as to who they were, or what they carried. To confront them in the street would be too obvious. An element of surprise was required, but he needed to avoid being seen by the angry dead for whom he would be a target.

Lifting the roof hatch behind the dome, he slipped onto the steel ladder that would take him onto a ledge above the stage from where he could descend unseen to the rear service rooms. From below, he could hear the murmuring and muttering of the agitated crowd, who he was sure meant him harm. He knew that to face them or to attempt subterfuge by magic would be his end. He also knew his strength was rapidly decaying again, and what little he did have he would need to challenge Norton. Having descended to floor level, Masterton made his way faltering through one of the darkened service rooms and through to the passage that led to the ballroom's rear doors.

Outside, Norton, assisted by his Aunt Mary pulled at the sheet of plywood that covered those same doors.

PC Bardon's beat had taken him a quarter of a mile or so into the town. He continued to advise those on the street to return to their homes, but the darkness, the lightning and the rumbles of thunder seemed to elicit an excitement in some. He needed to get to the telephone box near the railway station and call Tara to make sure she was alright. Several people had told him about the strange procession and the gathering outside the old Empire Ballroom, and that would be his next port of call. He turned and looked towards the seafront. From his vantage point he could see the dome atop the ballroom and the strange blue almost purple glow that illuminated it, something he had seen before. But above it, as if projected onto the lowering clouds was a symbol, an inverted five-pointed star surrounded by a circle, and at its centre a reversed 'Z'. He turned and continued to walk, the feeling now even stronger that he must call Tara making him increase his pace. In the distance he could hear the chimes of an ice cream van, but they were distorted and wavering like a warped gramophone record.

Opening the door to the phone box, he paused for a second to allow the smell of stale tobacco and urine to abate in the cold night air. With a coin at the ready he lifted the receiver and placed it to his ear, expecting to hear the familiar buzz of the dial tone, but instead he heard a man's maniacal laughter. Slamming the receiver down and pushing the door of the kiosk wide open, he began to run. He had to get to the Beach View Hotel and Tara, now!

As he turned to continue his panicked run, he darted down a side street and was blinded by a pair of headlights coming from the opposite direction. He stopped and shielded his eyes with his right hand and stepped back as far as he could on the pavement.

On the road a car pulled up level with him. Uncovering his eyes and blinking, Bardon looked down upon a Morris Minor Panda car. The driver's window steadily lowered and a familiar and welcome voice called out, 'Steve, it's Murray. The station called me at home, said you hadn't checked in when you should have done. And given the number of calls they've had tonight about strange things happening in the town, they asked me to start my shift early and come out to find you.'

Bardon bent down and pulled the door handle towards him. The door clicked open. 'Well, Murray, I'm certainly glad to see you! Move over. Based on your recent track record, I'm driving!'

From the rear seat, a woman spoke. 'Good evening, PC Bardon.'

Rita Rawlson leant forward as Bardon turned his head, their faces a little too close for comfort. The young constable turned away.

'Good evening, Rita. I hope you haven't done anything to cause PC Murray to put you in the back of a police car?' Then he engaged first gear and pulled away.

'Not in the slightest, handsome. I flagged him down. I want to help the town. Apart from which, PC Murray didn't think it a good idea for me to be wandering the streets tonight.'

Bardon turned left at the top of the road and left again down the next side street towards the seafront, indicating left to travel east in the direction of the Beach View Hotel. 'And Murray is right, Rita. If you don't want to go home, I think you should stay with us. I don't think our superiors would question that, given what's happened to you over the past few days. I just need to stop off at the hotel to make sure Tara's alright.'

Rita leaned forward again as if she needed to be close to Bardon's ear, and in a voice, which was almost a whisper, said, 'Oh no, PC Bardon, she's not there. I saw her not long before we stopped to pick you up. She was with that Craig Norton and that Madame Volatska woman. They were heading towards the old Empire Ballroom, carrying a box or something.'

Bardon changed the direction indicator to right and waited for a moment for a vehicle travelling west along the promenade to pass. As it did, the headlights of the Morris illuminated the side of an ice cream van. Its resurrected driver turned to look at them, smiled and turned on the chimes, a sound so incongruous on that night of evil that Bardon shuddered and paused before pulling out. As he did so, the radio in the Panda car came alive with a call for a unit to attend reports of people attempting to break in at the rear of the old Empire Ballroom.

## Chapter 53

Behind the Empire Ballroom, Craig Norton and his aunt, Mary Sharp, stood at either end of the plywood sheet that covered the rear doors. They were about to pull it away from the frame to which it had been lightly nailed when they were caught in the beam of two headlights above which a blue beacon rotated. They let go of the edges of the plywood. Tara moved to Craig's side.

Bardon was the first to alight from the vehicle.

'Mr Norton, Mrs Sharp, I know things are a little, shall we say, *odd* at the moment, but I'm not sure I can condone forcing entry to private property.'

No sooner had the words left Bardon's mouth than the whole scene was illuminated by a flash of lightning directly above them. The ground shook as an explosive bang tore through the cold air. Bardon looked up at the strange blue almost purple glow that hung above the ballroom and at the now familiar symbol seemingly projected upon the clouds. Norton stood by the constable's side and looked to the sky.

'PC Bardon, this place is the centre of all this evil. Inside are the dead of fifty years ago; many are those that perished in a fire here and want revenge. A pound to a penny Nathaniel Masterton is here to raise his master, and tonight will be the night unless I stop it. And I'm the only one that can. I have a plan I need to execute, and soon.'

Tara Jones smiled sweetly at Steve Bardon. The spell on her was weakening and she realised who she was actually in love with. Taking Bardon's hand, she stood on tiptoe and kissed him on the cheek. 'He's right, Steve. He must carry out his plan tonight, or else the consequences for the town could be very serious. It might even mean we would have to delay our wedding!'

For a few seconds, Bardon was silent and just stared at the gorgeous girl who held his hand. 'Tara, are you serious?'

Tara squeezed his hand harder. 'Yes, Steve!'

Bardon pulled her close against him. 'In that case, let me give Mr Norton a hand to remove that wood. What are we hanging about for!'

Murray stood by the Panda car with Rita Rawlson at his side. She called out, 'If Masterton's in there, you're going to need me!'

In the gloom, Nathaniel Masterton waited.

Debbie Barry stood at the window of the upstairs nursery in her house. The sight of the empty cot was a wrench to her soul, but there was still hope that soon her beloved son would once again be sleeping peacefully in that room. One man had given her hope, a man who was dead, a man she should have been fearful of: Frank Chapley. Why should she be fearful of a dead man who offered her hope, the dead man whose presence she now associated with a feeling of calm. A week ago, she would have laughed and dismissed as rubbish the suggestion that such contact with the deceased was possible. But now she knew that it was and it wasn't the negative encounter portrayed in so many stories and films.

She was just about to draw the curtains on the increasingly dark and threatening evening, when, looking down onto the wet pavement below, she saw him, Frank Chapley, unmistakable, but now naked. He raised an arm and with the middle finger of a bony hand, beckoned to her. Debbie raced downstairs, threw on her coat and slipped her most sensible shoes upon her feet, then unlatched front door. Less than thirty seconds since she had seen him, she was standing in front of the dead man she had hoped she would see again.

Chapley held out a hand, which Debbie took in hers, a hand that was icy cold, the thin skin making it feel like the hand of a skeleton, a skeleton that was now gently pulling her away from her house. 'Come on, young lady, there is somewhere we need to be.'

Moira Taggart felt cold and tired. She switched on both bars of the small electric fire in her front room, followed by the radio, which by the time she had sat down in her favourite chair and pulled a shawl over knees had warmed up. The gentle waves of classical music filled the room. Moira's eyelids became heavy and she drifted into a state midway between wakefulness and sleep.

The music faded, the radio crackled and a man's voice spoke through the little set: 'Moira, it's tonight. Your work is done. Bless you, lovely lady. And thank you.'

Moira smiled, her mind drifted, and seconds later she fell into a deep and contented sleep.

## Chapter 54

Behind the old Empire Ballroom, Rita Rawlson had taken Craig Norton aside. 'Craig, I have an idea. Masterton will still be under the impression that I am one of his: his servant, as it were. He wants that chest you have there. He tasked me with helping to return it to him. I'm guessing it's the contents of that chest that he wants and not the chest itself. If we empty it, maybe hide the contents in the police car, I can take the empty chest, find Masterton, and distract him. He's bound to be close by. He'll know we're here for sure, and my bet is that he's already in the ballroom waiting.'

And of course, he was. Hidden in the room at the rear of the ballroom, waiting and listening. He'd heard the sound of the sheet of plywood being slid to one side, then the swoosh of the doors it had covered being opened. From behind him, the murmuring of the crowd of the dead was becoming louder. Fear was not an emotion he had felt for many decades. But he felt it now. Some of that crowd wanted revenge, and most likely a dramatic ceremonial revenge, culminating in his destruction. He heard footsteps.

PCs Bardon and Murray stood either side of the open door while Rita Rawlson took a few steps inside. For a moment, she paused and listened to the murmuring that came echoing down the dark corridor ahead of her. Placing the empty chest upon the ground, she called out, 'Masterton. Are you here? It's your servant, Rita Rawlson. I have what you were seeking.'

From the shadows beside her, there was shuffling, the sound of footsteps upon debris. Next to her stood Masterton. Ignoring Rita, he stooped down to pick up the chest, but as he did, Rita squatted down and placed her ample behind upon it.

'Come on, Rawlson. Shift. You've done well and will be rewarded.'

Rita remained seated. 'Yes, and I think we should discuss that reward before I hand over something that is clearly of such immense value to you.'

'But Rawlson, you're supposed to be my bloody servant!'

Outside, while the two constables stood guard, Craig Norton and Tara Jones had bundled the contents of the chest from the seat of the Panda car into their open arms and made their way to the front of the ballroom where the last of the dead were making their way inside. The smell of seared skin made Tara retch.

'Come on, Tara. Keep going. I need to get this stuff inside the ballroom and onto the stage. I hope Rita's alright. Who would have thought I would need *her* help!'

The dead seemed disinterested by the intrusion of the young couple, more interested in each other and the blue almost purple light that was spreading slowly down from the high-domed ceiling.

Norton deposited the items held in his arms upon the stage and relieved Tara of what she carried. Grabbing a small dilapidated table from in front of the stage, he climbed the few steps and placed it centrally upon the decaying wooden structure. 'Tara, up here, fast. There's no time to lose!'

By the time she reached his side, Norton had already begun to arrange the items so essential to the ritual he was about to perform upon the table. In his hand was the book that contained all he needed to know about the ceremony, including how to arrange the ritualistic items. The black cloth was spread upon the table, in its centre, the skull was placed facing away into the restless crowd beyond. To its side was placed the jar of ashes. Behind it the book, open at the page upon which was the incantation he would need to use.

Norton turned to face Tara. 'I don't know how much longer we can hold out. We have to assume that as she's not with us; that Rita is with Masterton.'

Tara reached out and took Norton's hand. 'This can't work, Craig. They demand a sacrifice: a baby.'

'We have no option but to try, Tara. This is my only chance. Tomorrow it will be too late. Fifty years have passed. The evil of those years will consume this town, it will spread like an infection, consume the good that remains.' From his coat pocket, Norton took a small torch which he flicked on and shone at the incantation upon the page of the book.

From behind him, a familiar voice called out, 'Norton, you'll want this, won't you?' Through the gloom, the friendly face of Steve Bardon appeared. In his hand he held the writhing cloth bag that seemed to be desperately trying to escape his grasp. Tara took the bag from him but, struggling to hold it, it fell to the floor and writhed and wriggled its way to the feet of Craig Norton.

For a few seconds, Tara stared into Steve Bardon's eyes.

'I love you, Steve. Sorry, I'm so very sorry!' Her emotions ran high, but this was not the moment for romantic gestures. She needed to be practical. 'Have you seen Rita since she went inside?'

The young PC shook his head. 'Not since we were all together outside. I sent Murray in after her.'

From the rear of the ballroom a scream rang out. Bardon turned and ran into the gloom behind the stage. Following the guidance of the book that rested upon the table, Norton picked up the glass jar, unscrewed the lid, and carefully sprinkled the ashes it contained around the skull. Then, taking a lighter from his shirt pocket, he lit the black candle. He was aware that the faces of the crowd gathered in the strangely illuminated ballroom were now turned to face him.

Standing outside the rear of the ballroom, Mary Sharp had heard the scream, and, shrugging away any sense of fear, she stepped into the darkness through the open rear door. It took a moment for her eyes to adjust to the inky darkness within, but when they did, the face that loomed in front of her was unmistakable: Nathaniel Masterton.

'Madame bloody Volatska! If you're looking for that Rawlson woman, you're wasting your time. She tried to cheat me, so I've dealt with her. And that pathetic copper didn't even try to help her. Just ran off. Didn't see that coming, did you? Bloody fortune-teller, my foot! If I had time, I'd deal with you too, but I have something I need to do. I suggest you go back the way you came and keep your nose out of this. And, you'll be lucky if you see that nephew of yours again!'

Masterton sank back into the gloom of the corridor ahead of him.

Mary Sharp took a packet of cigarettes and a lighter from her handbag, pulled a cigarette from the pack, lit it, then held the lighter high to shed some light on her surroundings. Turning to her left, she could see that a doorway opened onto another room, the room from which she guessed Masterton had come from. Moving closer, she could see something lying in the middle of the floor. Lowering the lighter and crouching down, she could see it was Rita Rawlson, her face deathly pale, her eyes wide open, unblinking. Swallowing back the bile that rose in her throat, Mary sat down upon the floor as a wave of nausea swept over her.

On the stage of the ballroom, Craig Norton stood behind the small table, his face appearing as pale as that of the skull. Close by stood Tara, her right hand reached out to hold Norton's left, a mixture of emotions making her want to both smile and cry. She had to trust Norton, but she wished Steve Bardon, the man she loved, was by her side. The crowd before the stage had ceased their murmuring, and a hush had now fallen within the ballroom. The candle flickered, the bag writhed and rattled.

Craig Norton, in a strong theatrical voice, began the invocation:

*Thy shall rise again among the living. Come back to us. Come back to us that we may take from you the strength we need this night to bring back your brothers and sisters to walk among mankind and spread our word. Oh, Master of the Dark, Simon Clark-Mathos, come back. Through us you shall live again.*

The ballroom was filled by the strange blue almost purple light, which was steadily growing brighter. The crowd had begun to chant, their voices joined in a strange but beautiful harmony. 'Oh, brother of the dark, come back.'

From beside the stage, Masterton ran onto the dance floor and turned to face the stage. Raising both arms in the air, his fists clenched, he shouted to Norton, but his words could barely be heard above the chanting of the crowd. 'Norton, you bastard. You think you're clever, but you're summoning the Master. He will destroy you for disturbing him. But not until he has granted me even more years to support his cause. Then he will renew the curse, not to come in another fifty years' time, but now and for all eternity. This town will become overwhelmed by evil!'

Norton took Tara's hand and squeezed it tight, then he repeated the last part of the invocation, his voice now very loud and powerful:

Oh, brother of the dark, come back. Through us you shall live again.

The light in the ballroom began to turn to white, gradually increasing in brightness over the space of a minute. The dilapidated and long disused ballroom was restored from the roof down to its former glory. The crowds of the dead now appeared alive, their faces unburnt, their attire smart. From underneath the stage, an organ rose upon which an organist played a dance tune once popular during the 1920s. Then darkness engulfed the scene, the sound of the organ fading.

A blinding flash came from behind Norton and Tara and for a moment there was silence. As the flash faded, a bright blue light formed on the stage, casting a shadow thirty feet tall on the rear wall of the ballroom, the shadow of a cloaked man. Norton turned to face the rear of the stage, releasing Tara's hand, which joined her other hand to clutch her stomach as she doubled over in agony, collapsing onto the stage, unnoticed by Norton.

The crowd began to chant, a chant that grew louder by the second, 'Oh Master, you have returned to be among us.'

Seemingly, floating ten feet above the stage, Norton's eyes fixated on the face of Simon Clark-Mathos. Directly in front of the stage stood Masterton, a broad smile on his face. He called out in a voice that echoed around the ballroom, 'Master, I seek forgiveness. It was this fool who disturbed your timeless slumber. Destroy him. Do what is your will in this town. I beg more life that I might serve you for maybe another hundred years or more.'

Clark-Mathos looked down upon the smiling figure of Masterton, who now held in front of him the medallion depicting the symbol of the Brethren of the Visiting Spirits. The air in the ballroom began to vibrate, the dance floor vibrating in sympathy. Clark-Mathos pointed at Masterton and took a deep breath. 'It's you that is the fool, Masterton. You destroyed many of these people's lives by allowing them to burn in this very place. These people were my followers and could have spread the word further. Instead, the Brethren of the Visiting Spirits became associated with mass death and I could not now condone yet another, especially that of an innocent. I see now how wrong I was and I release the town from the curse. As for you, Masterton, let these people take the revenge for which they have waited so long.'

The crowd surged forward and in seconds, Masterton was engulfed within their ranks. Clark-Mathos lowered to the stage and cast his hand over the table. The candle flame became an intense ball of light, unaffected by the breeze that blew away the sprinkled ashes.

On the floor, beside the table, the writhing cloth bag split open and human bones spilled out. Then they gathered together, first the bones of the feet, then the legs, the hips, the backbone, and rib cage. Then the arms and the shoulder blades, then, finally the hands, which reached out and took from the table the skull which they placed atop the backbone. The arms lowered to the side of the now complete skeleton, and from the crown of the head downwards, flesh began to cover the body, and long dark wet hair formed. A white dress steadily covered the body whose naked form could still be seen underneath the soaking material.

But then, as fast as it had formed, the sodden dress was replaced by a pretty, floral-patterned one held by a bow around the waist. The hair was no longer wet but flowed beautifully in a gentle breeze, wavy, dark. The girl turned to Craig Norton, smiled, and mouthed the words 'thank you' then walked to the edge of the stage, descended the few steps to the dance floor and walked slowly to the door at the front of the ballroom.

Next to the table, Tara Jones lay still clutching her stomach, the cells that had been multiplying in her womb for the last few days now ejected in a bloody mess beneath her skirt. Clark-Mathos looked down upon his own daughter, tears running down his cheeks. He turned to face Norton.

'She will be alright. You must make sure she is taken home soon and looked after. I thank you for bringing this to my attention beyond the veil, the plight of the town and of my very own offspring. Masterton is gone, as I must go too.'

The ballroom was plunged into an inky darkness for a few seconds until the clunk of electrical switches could be heard, and the reassuring glow of lamps lit the balconies, the stage and dance floor. Clark-Mathos was gone, along with the crowd, and Masterton. In the centre of the dance floor stood the naked Frank Chapley and next to him, Debbie Barry.

From the door beside the stage, Mary Sharp appeared, carrying the chest, where from within could be heard the sound of a baby crying. She walked up to Debbie Barry, placed the chest on the dance floor and opened the lid. Debbie fell to her knees and scooped her son up in her arms, tears of joy flowing down her face and onto his. She turned her head to one side to thank Frank Chapley, but he was gone, now lying on a mortuary table, wrapped in a sheet that was much the worse for wear. PC Murray stood by Rita Rawlson. He had covered her with his police tunic and carried out the resuscitation technique taught to him at the Police Training College. She had coughed and wheezed, then breathed deeply.

She smiled at the young constable and in a strained voice said, 'Next time a good-looking lad does that to me, I hope it's under happier circumstances.'

Debbie Barry held her baby tight; she would not let him out of her sight for days.

Mary Sharp climbed the stage steps and walked to where her nephew was standing, smiled, reached into her handbag, took out the packet of cigarettes, dropped them onto the stage and ground them down with her right foot.

Craig looked at her, a little astonished. 'Mary, are you alright?'

She smiled. 'I'm fine, Craig. You see, while everything was going on in here, I had, well, I suppose what you might call a vision, a vision of my future. I was lying in a hospital bed, a doctor and a nurse stood by my side. I was coughing and was weak. I heard the doctor saying to the nurse, "In another twenty years' time people will recognise fully the danger of smoking. But in the meantime, many more will die in this horrible way." So that's it, Craig, no more smoking for me.'

Steve Bardon lifted Tara from the stage and kissed her gently on the cheek. He needed to take her to the warmth and safety of her rooms at the Beach View Hotel.

She locked up at his face and whispered, 'Sorry, Steve. I love you.' She closed her beautiful eyes and fell asleep.

On the small table upon the stage, the candle had become nothing more than a thin coating of wax over the candle holder. The book lay on the floor, closed. Norton picked it up, and although he had seen it so many times before, he turned it over and over in his hands as if it was the first time he had seen it. Then he turned to face his aunt. 'Mary, put this in your bag. We will probably never need to use it again in anger. When and if I come to put pen to paper and describe the incredible events of the last few days, it will be invaluable to me.'

# Chapter 55

Sitting outside, upon a bench opposite the ballroom, was a fisherman. A fisherman whose daughter had been taken fifty years before, taken by Nathaniel Masterton of the Brethren of the Visiting Spirits when she was barely twelve years old, and sacrificed by drowning, her skull used for their evil rituals. Sometime later, the police had found the rest of her skeleton in an outbuilding behind a terraced house in Stonypool where Simon Clark-Mathos was said to have held dark masses. The bones had been given back to the father, who rather than give them the interment at sea as had been his plan, had kept them close by until his own death twenty-five years before. Many items relating to his life as a fisherman had been donated by a friend to be displayed in Moira Taggart's museum.

Through the front doors of the ballroom, came the drowned girl, now looking beautiful as she had done in life, and although a stiff offshore breeze was now blowing, her hair waved only gently, her dress remaining still. Walking up behind the bench, she put a hand on her father's shoulder. He turned his head, then stood as she made her way around the bench to stand by his side. He took her hand and the pair turned to face the sea. Then they walked slowly to the steps that descended to the beach, taking one careful step at a time until they stood upon the stones and sand below, which they crossed until they stood at the water's edge. There they faded until, with a flash of light, they vanished, appearing again at that very same moment in front of Moira Taggart as she slumbered in her favourite chair in the front room of her bungalow where the electric fire glowed in the darkness and the radio played some dance tune that she knew from her past. She opened her eyes, the lids heavy from sleep, and a gentle smile formed upon her lips.

The fisherman and his daughter came close. 'Moira Taggart, you have a good soul. We both thank you. Now come with us, be *with* us, away from the ravages and cruelty of time.' Moira closed her eyes, and a moment later she was standing by father and daughter, looking back upon her earthly body that still smiled sweetly.

A few seconds later, the overstressed adaptor that was plugged into the ancient two-pin socket on the skirting board used to power the radio, the electric fire, and the table lamp, flashed, and a little plume of smoke rose into the air. The radio crackled and the room was plunged into darkness.

On the promenade, Big Tony stood with Julie, the barmaid, looking at the front of the old Empire Ballroom. He put an arm around her shoulder and when she didn't flinch or pull away, he took his chance. 'Hey Julie, you're really quite a babe, aren't you? Fancy going out for a drink with me one night?'

From behind them came a familiar voice. 'So long as it's at my pub where I can keep an eye on you!' The pair turned towards a smiling Ken Lomes, who added, 'Julie, thank goodness you're alright. You just disappeared!'

Julie hugged the usually bad-tempered landlord. 'I'm fine, Ken. Those weird people, two of them, came into the pub and led me away. That's why we should have locked the doors earlier.'

Ken smiled. 'I know and I'm sorry. With all that was going on, we really shouldn't have opened at all. By the way, I think you *should* have a drink with Tony. You actually make a lovely couple.'

Julie grinned and put an arm around Big Tony's waist. 'Well Tony, if the offer's still open, I would love to have a drink with you.' Then she winked. 'Maybe you can tell me why they call you Big Tony!'

In the distance the chimes of an ice cream van faded to be replaced by the sound of a paddle steamer's steam whistle giving a short blast close by.

Big Tony turned in the direction of the sound. 'Weird shit, eh?'

In their house a mile to the west of the town, Sid and Margaret sat watching television. Sid had closed the living room curtains against the darkening night and the flashes of lightning. Their television viewing had been interrupted during the evening by interference, but now the picture was steady and clear. Sid parted the curtains just enough to look out into the night.

'I reckon it was that strange weather, Margaret. It seems to have cleared now. So has the picture. There's a film I want to watch on ITV in ten minutes. I'll go and make us both a drink.'

Steve Bardon had taken an exhausted Tara Jones home in the Panda car, which he had then reluctantly entrusted to PC Murray for the rest of his shift. After a hot bath and a couple of brandies, Tara slipped into bed while Steve Bardon sat in a chair by her side.

As Tara turned over to make herself comfortable, her hand touched something on the pillow next to her, a piece of note paper, upon which were written a few lines. She tried to focus upon it, but the fatigue and the brandy had made her vision blurry. She rolled over again and held out the note to Steve Bardon.

'I can't imagine what this is or how it got here, Steve. Can you read it out to me?'

Steve Bardon took the sheet of notepaper and held it up to the weak light of the bedside lamp and began to read:

*Tara, I'm sorry.*

*Within a year, you will carry another child. You're now with a man more loyal and steadfast than I could have ever hoped to be.*
*Someday, we shall meet again, but not for a great many years, I think. Remember when we first met, and try not to think badly of me.*
*May you always be the smiling, beautiful woman you have become.*

*Your father,*
*Simon Clark-Mathos.*

As Tara drifted into sleep, a tear rolled down her pretty cheek.


## Chapter 56

When the sun rose, the folk of Stonypool opened curtains and doors upon a fresh new day. Overnight the cloud had cleared and a bright and frosty morning seemed to have cleansed the town. Craig Norton sat with his aunt, Mary Sharp, drinking coffee in the now smoke-free kitchen of her flat. In a few hours' time he would pack his bags and return to London and his job. He had much to tell family, friends and eventually many more, when he wrote of his time in Stonypool, in the book he intended to write. His aunt would miss him. They had built a special bond during the time he had spent with her.

Tara awoke early and in good spirits. The sight of a still-uniformed PC Steve Bardon asleep in the chair next to her bed made her smile. Next time he would sleep in her bed, she was sure of that.

Rita Rawlson had been taken to hospital the previous night but was seemingly suffering no ill effects when she awoke, apart from feeling a little groggy after some drugs that had been administered. What she really wanted was a couple of vodkas, but not alone this time. She would visit her husband's best friend, Ken Lomes, when she was discharged, and try and smooth things over.

Big Tony unlocked the door of Seashells Cafe, switched on the coffee percolator, and started frying sausages while he thought about Julie. He really had taken a shine to the young barmaid.

Ken Lomes sat in the saloon bar of the Ship and Anchor, performing a duty he knew he must face, to write a speech that he would read out at the funeral of his best friend, Dennis Rawlson.

Moira Taggart was found later that morning by the young woman who visited her a couple of times a week to help out with cleaning and shopping. And although she was shocked and upset, the smile still upon the old lady's face suggested her final moments had been peaceful.

PC Murray had returned to the police station in the early hours of the morning, the Morris Minor Panda car unmarked. A member of the ambulance crew from the previous night had contacted the duty inspector at the station to say how impressed he was with Murray's action, and that it had saved Rita Rawlson's life.

By mid-morning, the town was busy for a late autumn day, with shops open and tradespeople carrying out their duties. Among those delighted to be out in the bright sunshine was young mother

Debbie Barry, who proudly pushed the pram in which lay her son along the High Street.

In the small yard behind the grocery store, the ice cream van was parked, its chimes silent. It would take some months before the memories of what had happened to that little seaside town in those few days at the start of winter began to fade, but life did return to normal.

A long cold winter gave way to an increasingly warm spring, and Stonypool prepared for the summer season. Rita Rawlson had taken over management of the pier in honour of her husband, assisted by his old best friend, landlord Ken Lomes, who had found he actually liked having Rita around, especially as she was willing to spend spring evenings behind the bar of the Ship and Anchor when his barmaid, Julie, left to help Big Tony at Seashells Cafe. That was after Tony bought the ice cream van and took over the round.

A pregnant Tara Jones had employed a girl from the village to help her prepare the Beach View Hotel for the summer guests. In the girl's pocket was an invitation to the wedding of Steve Bardon and Tara Jones.

On a particularly warm and bright day, Steve and Tara took a stroll towards the cafe. Driving a repaired Morris 1100 Panda car from the west was PC Murray, who upon seeing the couple, turned his head and waved, mounted the pavement, and ran the little Morris into a signpost.

Yes, all seemed back to normal in Stonypool, although the state of the old Empire Ballroom continued to be an item on the agenda of many council meetings.

## Chapter 57

Fifty years later, Craig Norton returned to Stonypool. He had visited many times since that strange period, so many years ago, to visit his aunt to whom he had become very close. That was before her death some twenty years ago. Today, he had returned to place some flowers upon her grave at the parish church. It was again the end of the season in Stonypool, but it had been a long, hot summer. Even in late October, the sun warmed the day, but the evenings reminded the people of the town that winter was fast arriving. In an attempt to make the most out of those final warm days, an ice cream van was parked on the promenade opposite the old Empire Ballroom, which had been restored to its former splendour. Now a busy venue and a great bonus to the local community, it was now host not only to dances, but plays, shows, and talks

As Craig queued at the ice cream van, he became engaged in conversation with a man standing in front of him. 'Good to see that the old Empire Ballroom has been restored. I did worry that it would be demolished and some awful structure put in its place.'

The man smiled and held out a hand to shake Craig's. 'I could never let that happen, so five years ago, I bought it for a ridiculously low price from the council on the proviso that I restored it for community use. So what you see in front of you is all down to me.'

Craig Norton shook the man's hand warmly. 'Well, you saved a wonderful building. May I ask your name, by the way? Mine's Craig Norton.'

By now, the man was at the front of the small queue. 'Oh, just a 99 with two flakes for me please.'

Then to Craig he said, 'Well, you see, I felt I had a duty. I have a connection with the place. When I was a baby, I was taken, and the old Empire Ballroom is where I was found a couple of days later – under very strange circumstances apparently. My name? Yes, it's David, David Barry.'

Craig ordered his ice cream from the van and moved to stand where he had a better view of the ballroom. Looking towards the front doors he saw behind them a man he thought he recognised. A man wearing a brown warehouse coat. David Barry had joined him.

'Well, David, you've done an amazing job. Yes, some very strange things happened here fifty years ago.'

The man in the warehouse coat waved from behind the glass doors. Craig Norton waved back. 'He seems like a friendly chap. He looks familiar, although I'm sure I can't know him?'

'Who's that, Craig?'

'The guy in the foyer with the brown warehouse coat on. He was waving.'

David Barry looked perplexed. 'I hope not, the place is locked up. There's nobody in there, I can assure you.'

The pair crossed the road together, ice creams in hand.

'Sorry, David, must have been a reflection. My old eyes aren't what they were.'

David chuckled.

But it was not a reflection. And as Craig Norton drew close to the steps at the entrance to the ballroom, the man behind the glass doors smiled and unbuttoned his coat, pulling it apart to reveal a chain around his neck, upon which hung a medallion in the form of a symbol that Craig Norton knew so well.

EIN HERZ FÜR AUTOREN A HEART FOR AUTHORS À L'ÉCOUTE DES AUTEURS MIA KAPΔIA ΓIA ΣYΓΓPA
HJÄRTA FÖR FÖRFATTARE UN CORAZÓN POR LOS AUTORES YAZARLARIMIZA GÖNÜL VERELIM SZÍV
CUORE PER AUTORI ET HJERTE FOR FORFATTERE EEN HART VOOR SCHRIJVERS TEMOS OS AUTOR
SZÍVÜNKÉRT SERCE DLA AUTORÓW EIN HERZ FÜR AUTOREN A HEART FOR AUTHORS À L'ÉCOUTE
INAÇÃO ВСЕЙ ДУШОЙ К АВТОРАМ ETT HJÄRTA FÖR FÖRFATTARE Á LA ESCUCHA DE LOS AUTOR
AUTEURS MIA KAPΔIA ΓIA ΣYΓΓPAΦEIΣ UN CUORE PER AUTORI ET HJERTE FOR FORFATTERE EEN H
YAZARLARIMIZA GÖNÜL VERELIM SZÍVÜNKÉRT SERCE DLA AUTORÓW EIN HERZ FÜR
SCHRIJVERS TEMOS OS AUTORES INAÇÃO ВСЕЙ ДУШОЙ К АВТОРАМ ETT HJÄRTA FÖR

# The author

Andrew Braeman was born in Mitcham, Surrey. He began a career in electronic repair in 1979, which has progressed into telecommunications. He is currently a senior radio engineer for Sussex and Surrey police.

He has lived on the south-east coast of England since 1998 since which time his interest in the paranormal has grown. He is now a member of the Society for Psychical Research. He has previously written short stories in the paranormal genre for the entertainment of friends. The Stonypool Curse is his first novel.

Andrew got married in 1990 but divorced in 2004. He has three adult sons and two grandchildren. Alongside writing, in his spare time Andrew enjoys reading, flying, amateur radio, and electronic restoration and repair.